Praise for E. D. Baker's

Tales of the Wide-Awake Princess

The Bravest Princess

"This clever, funny third Wide-Awake Princess tale is packed with action and a little romance." —*The Horn Book*

"Romantic, suspenseful, and charming, it's no wonder this series has so many fans." —Storytime Hooligans

Unlocking the Spell

"Readers will delight in the twists the author makes to the familiar tales, seamlessly weaving them into the plot." —*Kirkus Reviews*

"A good example of a quest for girls who are seeking something light and fun." —*Library Media Connection*

⸺ THE ⸺ Wide-Awake Princess

"This blend of romance, suspense, magic, and humor offers an entertaining, peppy fractured fairy tale." —*Booklist*

"Will be enjoyed by readers who like adventure with a touch of romance." —*School Library Journal*

Books by E. D. Baker

A Tale of the Wide-Awake Princess

The
Princess
and the Pearl

E. D. BAKER

BLOOMSBURY
NEW YORK LONDON OXFORD NEW DELHI SYDNEY

First published in the United States of America in March 2017
by Bloomsbury Children's Books
Paperback edition published in March 2018
www.bloomsbury.com

Bloomsbury is a registered trademark of Bloomsbury Publishing Plc

For information about permission to reproduce selections from this book, write to
Permissions, Bloomsbury Children's Books, 1385 Broadway, New York, New York 10018
Bloomsbury books may be purchased for business or promotional use. For information
on bulk purchases please contact Macmillan Corporate and Premium Sales Department at
specialmarkets@macmillan.com

The Library of Congress has cataloged the hardcover edition as follows:
Names: Baker, E. D., author.
Title: The princess and the pearl / by E. D. Baker.
Description: New York : Bloomsbury, 2017. | Series: Wide-awake princess
Summary: When Princess Annie's father and uncle fall ill, Annie and Liam must
set sail on dangerous seas full of sea monsters and magical creatures
to find the only cure, a giant pearl.
Identifiers: LCCN 2016022362 (print) • LCCN 2016046304 (e-book)
ISBN 978-1-68119-135-5 (hardcover) • ISBN 978-1-68119-136-2 (e-book)
Subjects: | CYAC: Fairy tales. | Princesses—Fiction. | Magic—Fiction. | Characters in
literature—Fiction. | BISAC: JUVENILE FICTION/Fantasy & Magic. | JUVENILE FICTION/
Fairy Tales & Folklore/General. | JUVENILE FICTION/Love & Romance.
Classification: LCC PZ8.B173 Pro 2017 (print) | LCC PZ8.B173 (e-book) | DDC [Fic]—dc23
LC record available at https://lccn.loc.gov/2016022362

ISBN 978-1-68119-612-1 (paperback)

Book design by Donna Mark
Typeset by Westchester Publishing Services
Printed and bound in the U.S.A. by Berryville Graphics Inc., Berryville, Virginia
2 4 6 8 10 9 7 5 3 1

This book is dedicated to my uncle,
Dr. Raymond Carnes, the sweetest and kindest man
I've ever known. We will miss him.

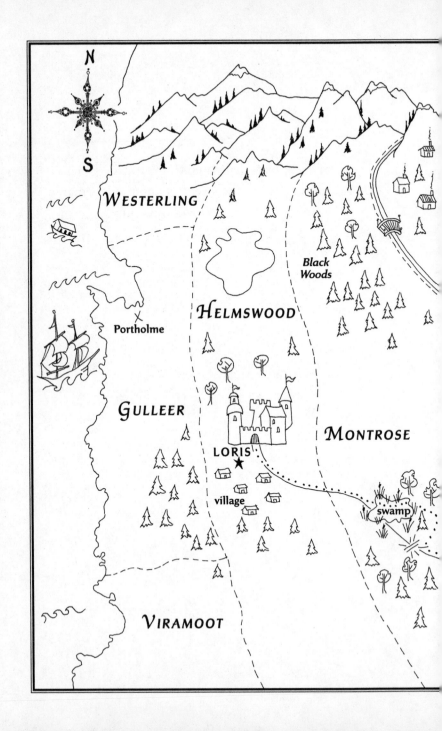

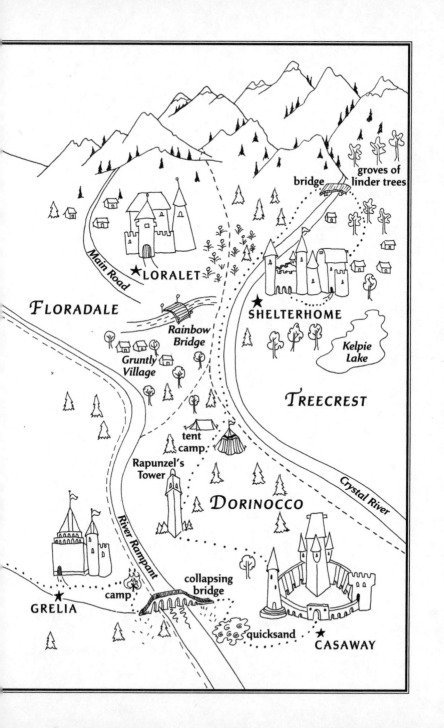

CHAPTER 1

PRINCESS ANNIE STEPPED into her chamber and glanced at all the trunks that servants had packed in her absence, preparing for her move to Dorinocco. Liam was about to be crowned king, which meant that Annie would always want to look her best. She was taking her nicer gowns and would have more made upon her arrival. She already knew that she would miss Treecrest, but the two kingdoms were close enough that she planned to visit often.

Annie had slipped off her shoes and was placing them by her bed when a disembodied head appeared in the corner. "Where have you been?" the face asked, scowling. Startled, it took Annie a moment to remember that the magic mirror was in that corner now.

"You left me all alone for days without telling me where you were going or when I'd see you again!" the face declared. "Why would you do that?"

"I'm sorry," Annie replied. "Liam and I didn't expect to leave when we did. I couldn't have told you where we were going because we didn't know until we got there. It wasn't an ordinary grand tour."

"You went on your grand tour!" said the face in the mirror. "No one told me that! All those ladies came to consult me about their love lives, and not one of them told me a thing!"

"So you weren't all alone!" said Annie. "Who came to see you?"

"Just a few people. Your sister came first, then Lady Patrice and Lady Cecily and Lady Clare and Lady Josephine and Lady Hortense and three kitchen maids named Ula, Bev, and Winnie. You wouldn't believe what they asked me!"

"I'm not interested in gossip," said Annie.

The face in the mirror looked outraged. "This isn't gossip! I'm just telling you about my conversations."

Annie turned away when she heard a knock on the door, opening it to admit servants carrying buckets of steaming water. She had worn the same clothes for the entire trip. They were so filthy now that she didn't want to sit on her bed or chair, so she waited while the servants filled the tub and set the screen in front of the magic mirror so he couldn't see past it. The face in the mirror grumbled, but Annie didn't care. All she could think about now was a nice hot bath and finally getting clean.

The moment the door closed, Annie disrobed and stepped into the tub. Although the water felt too hot at first, she eased her way in and sat back, letting the warmth relax her tired muscles. Within minutes, Annie felt better than she had in days. True, she had enjoyed a bath in the palace in Westerling, and gone swimming at the giants' island, but she hadn't felt truly safe and able to fully unwind until now.

Annie and Liam had been planning to sail along the coastline for their grand tour, but news of an evil wizard and the gift of magic postcards from a woods witch had sent them on an unexpected trip. If their lives hadn't been in danger wherever they went, they might have enjoyed it more, but they had visited places they hadn't known existed and made new and highly unusual friends. They had even visited Annie's uncle, Rupert, someone she had never met before. The grand tour had been shorter than she and Liam had planned, and not at all where they'd wanted to go, but it had been marvelous and exciting.

Annie glanced out the window. It was getting late in the day; she'd have to dress for supper in a little while. She had wanted to see her parents as soon as she got back, but they had been in a meeting and unable to see her then. Although she'd wondered what kind of meeting would have kept them from welcoming her and Liam, she was glad to have a chance to get cleaned up first. Liam had been eager to bathe as well, and had gone to the room he'd used before the wedding, hoping his clothes were still there.

Annie dozed until the water cooled enough to fully wake her. She washed then, scrubbing her skin and hair until the last vestiges of her trip were gone. After drying off, she put on an old peach-colored gown that wasn't good enough to pack, brushed her hair, and started for the door.

"Leaving without saying good-bye again?" said the face in the mirror.

"I'm just going to supper," Annie replied. "I'll be back soon."

"Just don't go on any long trips without telling me first," said the mirror.

Annie took a step back into the room. She hadn't been planning to take the magic mirror with her when she moved to Dorinocco, but maybe it wouldn't be a bad idea. The face in the mirror had been useful at times and she had almost started to like it. "Liam and I are going to Dorinocco," she said. "His father is stepping down and Liam is going to be crowned king. We'll be living there from now on. Would you like to come with us?"

"You were leaving without me? I knew something was going on when people packed up all your clothes! Of course I want to come! You may like tapestries of unicorns and flowers way too much and your singing makes me wish I could plug my ears, but being with you is a lot better than being with Queen Marissa. She was almost as horrible to me as she was to Snow White. That woman gave me no respect! I don't know how many times she threatened to toss me into the moat or a pit full of snakes. I hate snakes! They squiggle through the muck and leave ugly trails all over your nice, clean glass."

"Then you're welcome to come," said Annie. "I'll let the steward know that you need to be loaded on the cart before we leave." She had started out the door again when something occurred to her. Once again, she turned back to face the mirror. "I don't understand something. You can see what other people are doing all the time. When I was gone, why didn't you just look for me?"

"I tried," said the mirror. "But I could never find you. Magic doesn't work on you, remember?"

"I didn't realize it would block you from seeing me," Annie said. "I learn something new every day. I'll try to remember to tell you whenever I'm going away, if that will make you happy."

"Delirious," said the face, although it still looked grumpy.

On her way down the stairs, Annie thought about what the mirror had said. It hadn't occurred to her that the mirror couldn't see her when she was away, but then it wasn't really a surprise. Since the day the fairy Moonbeam gave Annie her one and only magical christening gift, she had been impervious to magic. Not only would magic bounce off Annie if someone tried to cast a spell on her, but everyone else's magic faded when she was nearby. Annie had thought this would always be true, and it wasn't until she received the magic postcards that she learned there was a form of magic stronger than the fairy kind. Dragon magic was the strongest of all. It was the one kind of magic that affected Annie as much as it did everyone else. It was the reason she and Liam had been able to use the magic postcards. It was also the reason they'd been able to come back home.

Annie was halfway down the stairs when people started to greet her. The entire time she was growing up, she'd been shunned by relatives, courtiers, and anyone made more attractive or talented through magic. After she broke her sister's curse, her family had warmed to her and the others hadn't avoided her quite as much. However, since the day of her wedding, these same courtiers seemed to be drawn to her. Not only had she brought the fairies to repair the damage to the castle, making up for the spells they had cast, but she had ended King Dormander's siege as well. What people seemed to remember the most, however, was the wedding the fairies had put on for her. They were still talking about it as they stopped her on the stairway.

"It was the most beautiful thing I've ever seen," one elderly courtier said, surprising Annie because the woman had never spoken to her before.

"I cried during your wedding, and I never cry! Not even when my dear Randolf died!" said another older woman.

"I still cry every time I think about it!" a third woman told her.

Unsure how to respond, Annie smiled and nodded and hurried down the stairs. The fairies had outdone themselves and it had been a beautiful wedding, but so many other things had happened since then that Annie felt as if the wedding had taken place long ago.

When Annie reached the great hall, it was as crowded and noisy as usual. Ewan, the young redheaded page, met her at the door. "Her Highness Queen Karolina asks that you sit at the high table from now on," he said. "This way, if you please."

Annie smiled after he turned away. The boy was so proud of his position and excited about what he was doing that she almost had to laugh. When she glanced at the dais, where her parents usually sat, she saw Liam waiting for her. Her parents weren't there, but she expected to see them any minute.

"Are Princess Gwendolyn and Prince Beldegard still in the castle?" she asked Ewan.

The page shook his head. "They left for Montrose two days ago. No one expects them back anytime soon."

Liam stood as Annie approached the dais. "You look...clean!" she said with a smile.

Liam laughed. "So do you! I feel much better now. It's amazing what a hot bath and clean clothes can do for a person. Now all I need is to sleep for about three days and I'll be back to normal."

"That sounds tempting," said Annie. "When did you want to go to Dorinocco?"

Liam pushed her seat in for her, then sat down, saying, "I suppose we should go as soon as possible. We have a lot to do if I'm to take over from my father. If we get a good night's rest tonight, we can leave early tomorrow morning."

"We still have to decide where we're going to send Clarence and your mother," said Annie.

"I know," Liam said, frowning. "The sooner we do that, the better."

Liam's mother, Queen Lenore, and his brother, Prince Clarence, had conspired to take over Annie's home kingdom of Treecrest. When the tiny spinning wheel they'd sent had made Gwennie's curse come true, Annie had found princes to wake her sister with a kiss. King Montague had locked his queen in a tower, but Clarence had run off to sea, returning with a nasty wizard who assisted in the siege of King Halbert's castle. Both Clarence and Queen Lenore were locked in King Montague's castle now, but Liam didn't want them anywhere nearby when he became king.

"Your Highness," said a voice at Annie's side. She turned to find Ewan waiting by her elbow. "Your mother,

8

Queen Karolina, has sent word that she and King Halbert will not be joining you for supper tonight. She asks that you come to the king's chamber after you've eaten."

"In that case, please tell the servers that they may begin," Annie told the page. No one ate before the king and queen arrived, but if they weren't coming …

Although the salmon was delicious, Annie couldn't do more than pick at her food. Something was wrong, she could feel it. Why else had her parents been unable to see her when she returned home? And why weren't they coming down to supper?

Seeing her unease, Liam ate quickly and they were soon headed upstairs to her father's chamber. Her mother met them at the door, ushering them to the chair where King Halbert was waiting. Annie had rarely seen him in his nightclothes before. Finding him dressed in a long robe and slippers made her worry even more. "What's wrong?" Annie asked as soon as she saw him. "Did something happen?"

"Your father isn't feeling well," said the queen. "It started last night. We had the doctor come see him today, but the man was worthless. He said he'd never seen anything like it before."

"Like what?" asked Annie. King Halbert sighed. "Your mother is making a big fuss over nothing. It's just a touch of stomach sickness, that's all. I wasn't able to eat last night or today, but I should be fine by tomorrow."

"That is not all it is and you know it!" declared the queen. "Show her your feet!"

"I'm not showing anyone my feet!" said the king.

"She's your daughter. She has the right to know what's going on!" the queen told him. "Show her your feet, Halbert, or I'll do it for you!"

King Halbert glared at his wife. When she glared back, he sighed and pulled his feet out of his slippers. Annie gasped. Her father's feet were blue. Not the kind of blue her feet turned when she'd been swimming in cold water too long, but the bright blue of a gown her mother often wore.

"Do they hurt?" she asked her father, kneeling down beside him.

"Not at all!" said the king. "They feel perfectly normal; they just look like I've been stomping blue grapes to make wine. I'm sure the color doesn't mean a thing. As soon as I get over this stomach sickness, I'll be up and around again."

Annie turned to her mother. "Can you send for another doctor?"

"No!" declared King Halbert. "They're all quacks! I don't want another of those blustering idiots near me! I'm fine, I tell you. I didn't have you come up here to fuss over me like your mother. I just want to hear about your trip. Moonbeam told us that you went by postcard. What an interesting way to travel! Pull up some chairs and tell me all about it. You might as well sit down, too,

Karolina. I know you're just as curious as I am, and I don't want you hovering over me any more tonight."

"Are you sure I can't send for anything for you?" said the queen.

"I'm positive," said the king. "Annie, start at the beginning. I want to hear everything!"

CHAPTER 2

THE NEXT MORNING, Annie and Liam woke as the sun came up, hoping to get an early start. After a quick breakfast of bread hot from the oven spread with butter and soft cheese, they went upstairs to see her parents. Annie's father was still in bed, but she was pleased to see that he was awake and looked better than he had the night before.

"How are you feeling, Father?" asked Annie.

"Much better," said the king. "Your mother gave me a tonic to help me sleep last night. My stomach isn't bothering me nearly as much today. I've already sent for breakfast, so there's no need to worry about me."

"If you're all right, Liam and I will be leaving this morning," Annie told him.

"I expected as much," her father told her. "Have a safe trip and come back for a visit as soon as you can."

Annie and Liam went to say good-bye to the queen

next. She had gone for an early-morning walk in the garden with some of her ladies-in-waiting. Although Queen Karolina had dark circles under her eyes, she assured Annie that everything was all right. "You're about to start a whole new life with your husband," said the queen. "I don't want you to worry about your father and me. We'll be fine. I'm sure your father was right. It was just a temporary indisposition. He'll be up and about today."

"If you're sure . . . ," said Annie.

"I am," said the queen. "I know King Montague is looking forward to your arrival. Don't keep Liam's father waiting any longer than you must."

Once the queen had dismissed them, Annie and Liam hurried to the courtyard, anxious to get started. Annie had sent money to pay for Otis and was looking forward to riding the gelding that day. With Liam riding Hunter, it felt almost like the trip they had taken from Dorinocco to the Garden of Happiness, only this time no one was chasing them, thankfully. They also had an escort of half a dozen knights to guard them, along with another half-dozen men guarding the wagon hauling Annie's belongings.

The magic mirror had been crammed into the wagon at the last minute, and Annie could still hear it grumbling as they crossed over the drawbridge. "Does the driver have to aim for every bump and pothole!" it called out.

"Let's ride ahead a bit," Annie said to Liam. "I really

don't want to hear the magic mirror complaining the whole way there. If I'd known it was going to be like that, I would have left it in my old bedroom."

"I heard that!" shouted the mirror.

Annie sighed and urged Otis to go a little faster. When the two horses trotted ahead, the six knights hurried to catch up, leaving half the group behind. Annie and Liam were still in the lead when they came to a crossroad where an elderly woman was sitting on a large rock.

Annie groaned and said, "Not that witch again! She must live close by. I see her every time I come this way."

"There you are!" the old woman shouted. A lizard slipped out of her mouth and a frog fell to the ground in a shower of rose petals. "Do you know how long I've been waiting for you? It's your fault I'm in this mess!" Spewing pearls like a messy eater dribbles crumbs, she made a horrible face when a snake slithered between her lips and tumbled to her lap.

"I didn't do anything to you," said Annie. "You wouldn't be in this mess if you didn't keep trying to cast spells on me."

"Whatever! It's going to end today," said the woman, and gagged on a pair of squirming salamanders. After wiping a rose petal off her tongue, she added, "I found a reversal spell that has got to work!"

The woman called out while waving her hands in the

air. Her words were garbled as toads, frogs, and a long, skinny snake with an arrow-shaped head slithered out of her mouth. A gray-green cloud swept toward Annie, roiled around in front of her, and washed back over the old witch.

"That should do it!" the witch declared.

When nothing squiggled from between her lips or fell from her mouth, she hopped up and down, clapping her hands in delight. Weeds near her feet began to rustle, but she didn't seem to notice.

"It worked!" she shouted. A big, warty toad emerged from the weeds. In one bound, it leaped at the witch, hitting her in the mouth. If her mouth hadn't been closed, the toad might have gone inside. Instead, it hit her lips and fell to the ground, landing on its back.

"What was that?" the witch cried. Rose petals that had fallen from her mouth just minutes before flew at her, pressing themselves to her lips.

Annie and Liam were almost past when the old woman screamed, "No!"

As pearls hurtled toward her face and a snake slithered onto her foot, the old woman clasped her hands over her mouth and ran into the forest.

"Let me guess," said Liam. "The old woman's reversal spell worked a little too well. No weird things are coming out of her mouth now. Instead, they're all trying to go back in!"

Annie nodded. "I think you're right. You know, if I were her, I'd become a hermit and never speak to anyone again!"

They could hear the wagon carrying Annie's possessions coming up behind them when they turned onto the road leading to Farley's Crossing. The small town had grown up around the only ferry that crossed the Crystal River and was a common destination for travelers. It took Annie and Liam's group more than an hour to get there. When they arrived, the ferry was loading and already nearly full. One of the knights rode up to tell the ferryman that the prince and princess wanted to cross and the surly man's eyes lit up.

"Do they now?" he said. He thought for a moment and named a price higher than anyone else would have to pay. When the guard nodded, the man chortled and turned to the passengers already on board. "You have to get off and wait for the next crossing!" he shouted at them.

The passengers got off without complaint, moving aside to let the new arrivals on while eyeing them with interest.

"This trip is so different from any we've ever taken together," Annie told Liam as they rode onto the ferry. "That was nice of the ferryman to let us get on now, and even nicer of all those people to get off for us."

"The ferryman did it because he knew he could get more money from us," said Liam. "The people did it because he was making them get off, plus they could watch us until the ferry leaves. Most of them have never seen a royal party before."

"Either way, it was nice of them," said Annie. "People don't usually treat me with that much respect."

"They will from now on," Liam said, his expression turning serious. "You're about to be Queen Annabelle of Dorinocco!"

"Have you decided what you want to do with Clarence and your mother?" asked Annie.

"I haven't decided where to take my mother, but I know what I want to do with Clarence. How do you think your uncle Rupert would feel about a permanent guest?"

"He might actually like it. They never have guests at the fortress and it would be someone for him to talk to other than his own soldiers."

"And Clarence wouldn't be able to get into much mischief," said Liam. "I think that's where we'll take him. We'll go first thing tomorrow. The sooner we get Clarence and my mother out of the castle, the happier I'll be."

The last knight had just ridden onto the ferry when the ferryman ordered his helpers to start across. Although Annie and Liam had used the ferry a number of times, this was the fastest trip they'd ever taken. They were halfway to the other side of the river when the wagon and the rest of the guards reached the dock behind them. Seeing the new arrivals, the ferryman grinned and rubbed his hands together.

"I have a feeling that those poor people who just got off the ferry will have to wait even longer now," said Liam. "The ferryman is already counting the money he's going to make when your wagon crosses, too."

"I'm sorry they'll have to wait, but I doubt they'll have to travel as far as those guards will today. How long before we reach the castle?" asked Annie.

"I was hoping we'd get there by nightfall, but we got a later start than we'd planned."

"At least we know that my father is all right," Annie said. "I couldn't have left if it had been something serious."

The ferry docked a few minutes later. Annie and Liam were the first to disembark, with the knights close behind. The party immediately turned south. Not wanting to stop until they reached the castle, they rode hard, but still didn't get there until after dark. They had to wait while guards lowered the drawbridge, which provided plenty of time for word of their arrival to spread.

"Good, you're here!" King Montague called from the steps when they entered the courtyard. "How was your grand tour?"

"Not what we'd planned, but wonderful nonetheless," Liam told him.

While accompanying the king to his private audience chamber, Annie and Liam told him about their travels. They sat at a table in the corner of the room, waiting for servants to bring supper for the hungry young couple. Annie and Liam were describing their visit with the giants when Queen Lenore swept into the room.

"I heard you were here!" she said. "I know it wouldn't occur to you to visit your mother, Liam, so I came to see you myself."

"I thought she was locked in the tower still," Liam said to his father.

"She's supposed to be, but she manages to convince the guards to let her out from time to time," said the king.

"I would replace the guards," said Liam.

"Who do you think you are, giving your king advice?" Lenore demanded.

"He has every right to make suggestions," said King Montague. "I'm abdicating in his favor. As soon as we can make the arrangements, Liam will be crowned the new king of Dorinocco."

Queen Lenore looked horrified. "What about Clarence?"

"I don't know how many times I've told you that Clarence will never be king!" the king said, getting angry. "After the stunts he's pulled, he's lucky I didn't have him beheaded! If it were up to me, I'd leave the both of you in the tower for the rest of your lives."

"You wouldn't do that to us, would you, Liam?" asked his mother.

"No, of course not!" Liam told her. Her expression turned triumphant until he added, "I don't want either of you in the kingdom when I rule. You are both being banished to places far from here."

"You can't do that!" cried Lenore. "I'm your mother!"

"And I will be king, so I can do whatever I think is best. I've already decided where I want to take Clarence. We'll be leaving in the morning."

Lenore gasped. "You can't take Clarence away from me! He's all I have left!"

"Not for long," said Liam. "Guards, take her back to the tower, and make sure she stays there this time if you don't want to end up in the dungeon yourselves. And inform my brother that he should pack some clothes, and include something warm. He's going to need it where he's going."

CHAPTER 3

TO ANNIE'S SURPRISE, Clarence was ready early the next morning. Two guards escorted him into the room where Annie and Liam were eating breakfast with King Montague. A servant followed behind, lugging a heavy sack.

"Will you look at this!" said Clarence. "I'm ready before you are."

"Someone would almost think you're eager to go," Liam said as he set down his mug of cider.

"You would be, too, if you were locked in with Mother," said Clarence.

Annie glanced from the king to Clarence. "I thought you had the entire tower!"

"We did, but that's very confining when I have to share it with Mother," Clarence told her. "Although I know she has my best wishes at heart, she informs me day and night that the world has wronged me and that I deserve so much more. Following her advice has gotten me nowhere except locked up with her! She's upstairs fuming right now. Let's go before she convinces yet another guard that she has something important to tell you, Father. That's how she usually gets out of the tower."

"We'll go as soon as Annie and I finish our breakfast and say good-bye to Father," said Liam.

"Father is sitting right next to you," Clarence declared. "Why don't you say good-bye to him now and save us all some time?"

King Montague looked exasperated when he said, "Have a seat, Clarence. They'll be ready in a few minutes."

The guards stood behind Clarence when he took a seat at the table. The servant waited by the door, still holding the sack, until Annie gestured for him to put it down and leave. She smiled behind her hand when Liam lingered over his breakfast, having second help-ings of everything. He had told her how much Clarence and the queen had tormented him over the years, and she knew Liam was enjoying this small amount of revenge.

Clarence watched Liam take every bite, glaring at him as if willing his brother to chew faster. When Liam finally sat back from the table, Clarence jumped to his feet. "Now can we go?" he asked.

Instead of answering his brother, Liam turned to

his father, saying, "We won't be gone long. Annie and I should be back in time for supper."

"Really?" said Clarence. "Then we must not be going very far."

"On the contrary," Liam told him. "We're actually going to travel to a place many miles from here."

Annie watched as Liam took a medallion out of his tunic. It was one she had owned for years, and she'd offered it to him to replace the medallion that King Lalidama of Westerling had taken. Rupert had given the first medallion to Liam, suggesting that he let people think it had magic so they wouldn't be interested in the postcards. Annie had agreed with Liam that letting Clarence see how the postcards worked would be a very bad idea.

After saying good-bye to the king and slipping on the warmest winter coat he owned, Liam told Clarence to put on his coat and pick up his bag. Clarence looked confused. "Why should I?" he asked. "It's warm out today and a servant can carry the bag to the courtyard for me."

"We're not going to the courtyard," said Liam.

Annie finished pulling up the hood of her winter coat before taking Liam's arm. Keeping one hand tucked in his pocket so he could hold the postcard, he held up the medallion with the other. "Hold on to your bag if you don't want to leave it behind," he told his brother. "And grab hold of my arm like Annie did."

One of the guards handed the bag to Clarence.

Although Clarence was reluctant to take his brother's arm, he tightened his grip when Liam announced, "Delaroo Pass," and rubbed the medallion three times.

Annie could feel Liam's arm tense, so she knew he was touching the postcard in his pocket. He was so convincing, however, that even she would have believed that he was using the medallion if she hadn't known better.

One moment they were in the warmth of the castle . . .

And the next they were standing on the wall of the fortress, looking down into the snow-covered mountain pass. It was a beautiful sight, but not one that Annie wanted to enjoy for long. She was already shivering, even though she was wearing her warmest coat. More than anything, she wished that she still had the fur coat that the guard had given her the last time they came to the fortress. Liam seemed fine, but Clarence had ignored his brother's suggestion and wasn't wearing a coat at all. He was shaking so hard when he tried to open his bag that Annie almost felt sorry for him.

A windowless tower stood only a few yards to their left. When Liam started toward the door into the tower, Annie followed him, hoping that it would open easily this time. Snow had fallen since the door was used last, making it as hard to move as it had been during their first visit. Annie started to help Liam clear the snow with her hands while Clarence pulled a coat from his bag and slipped it on. When Liam saw his brother standing there watching, he scowled and said, "Get over here and lend a hand! We'll get inside faster if three of us work."

"I don't do manual labor," Clarence said, looking scornful.

"You will if you want to get warm!" Liam told him.

"You and your wife are built for it," said Clarence. "I'm not."

"Annie, why don't you let Clarence take your place? I think he deserves a turn."

Annie moved out of the way, but Clarence didn't budge. When Liam saw him, he stopped working and moved to stand next to Annie. "You're going to have to learn that you're not the privileged person you think you are, Clarence. If you want to get along here, you'll do your fair share of the work." When Clarence still didn't move, Liam added, "I have a nice warm coat on. I can stand here for hours if I must."

"I can't," Annie whispered to him, tucking her hands, reddened from the cold, into the opposite sleeves.

Clarence looked defiant until his teeth were chattering so loudly that Annie could hear them. "Oh, all right," he said finally, and began to scoop the snow with his hands.

Annie and Liam let him work alone for a few minutes before moving to help. With the three of them working, they were soon done and Liam was able to open the door. When Clarence tried to push past him to go in first, Liam grabbed his arm, saying, "Ladies first! Go ahead, Annie."

She hurried inside and started down the stairs, remembering how dark the tower became once the door was shut. When Liam finally closed it behind them, Annie slowed down, feeling her way with her hand on the wall. Reaching the bottom, she announced, "This is the last step. If I remember correctly, the door is three paces forward and two paces to the right. Got it! Just a moment and you'll have more light." When she opened the door, light from open doorways lining the corridor made it easier for Clarence and Liam to follow her.

Annie was waiting for them to join her when she heard the deep barking of a large dog. The sound grew louder as the dog approached and she turned to face that direction. Liam and Clarence had joined her when the dog burst into view around a turn in the corridor. It was a huge dog with thick brown fur and it ran faster in its shuffling kind of gait when it saw Annie. Bracing herself, she waited for it. When the dog finally reached her, it set its paws on her shoulders, nearly knocking her down. Clarence shouted and ran behind Liam.

Annie laughed as the dog licked her face, spreading slobber across her cheek and down the side of her neck. "I'm glad to see you, too, Edda," she said, scratching the huge head.

"Get down now, girl," Liam told the dog.

Edda gave Annie's face one last lick. After sniffing Liam, the dog moved on to Clarence. "Keep that beast away from me!" Clarence shouted

Annie petted the dog's head, saying, "Edda isn't a beast. She's a troll dog."

"And she's particularly fond of Annie," said Liam.

"That's not a dog, it's a horse!" Clarence said, taking a step back.

"If you think she's big, wait until you see Big Boy!" Annie told him.

They turned at the sound of running footsteps. Three men rounded the corner, slowing when they saw Annie. "Is that you, Your Highness?" asked one of the men. "We didn't expect you back so soon."

Annie recognized the men, having met them during her last visit. "Hello, Captain Grant. We've come to see my uncle. Do you know where I might be able to find him?"

His two men exchanged glances while the captain cleared his throat. "He's probably in his bedchamber," the captain finally said. "Prince Rupert hasn't been feeling well lately."

"Is he worse than before?" Annie asked him. Her uncle hadn't been feeling well when they were there last time, but he hadn't been so ill that he'd had to stay in bed.

"I'm afraid so, Your Highness," said the captain. "He hasn't left his room in days."

"Then I must see him immediately," said Annie. "Liam, why don't you and Clarence stay down here? My uncle may not want company."

"But you're going," said Clarence.

"I'm not company. I'm family," Annie said as she began to follow the captain with Edda at her side.

❧

Annie was horrified when she saw her uncle lying in bed, his face nearly as pale as the pillows mounded up behind him. He turned to look at her as she walked into the room, but he was too weak to do more than give her a small smile. The huge dog lying by the side of the bed got to his feet as if to protect the prince. Edda sat down beside Annie.

"Uncle Rupert, what happened?" asked Annie.

"My ailment is progressing faster than I thought it would," said her uncle. "The blue has almost reached my chest."

"What blue?" said Annie, taking a step closer. "What are you talking about?"

"I didn't tell you about my disease?" her uncle asked. "I'm sorry, I thought I had. The pain is making my memory foggy. It started a few months ago. When I lost my appetite, I thought I had eaten bad salted cod. Then my feet started to turn blue. My appetite never really did come back, although some days have been better

28

than others, but the blue started to creep up my legs. Walking became more difficult the higher it spread. I'm glad you came back to see me. I won't be here in a few more weeks."

"Why do you say that?" said Annie. "I'm sure we can find a doctor to help you!"

"It's no use," Rupert told her. "My father had the same illness. My mother called on every healer in the kingdom, and none of them were able to do anything for him. When he died, he was blue all over."

"But you can't die from this!" Annie cried. "I don't want to lose you after we just met, and my father—" Annie's hand flew to her mouth, too appalled to say it out loud.

"What about your father?" Rupert asked, frowning.

"When I left the castle, my father had lost his appetite and his feet had just turned blue. He insisted that it was nothing, or I never would have left."

"Halbert has it as well?" Rupert said, struggling to sit up. "That's very bad news."

Annie hurried to the door with Edda shuffling beside her. When Annie saw that Captain Grant was speaking to another officer just down the hall, she called, "Captain, please have someone collect some of my uncle's belongings. I'm taking him back to the castle. And please ask Prince Liam and Prince Clarence to come join me. We'll be leaving soon."

Rupert settled back into his pillows and closed his eyes. "I'm not going anywhere. There's nothing that can be done for me, and I'd rather die in my own bed. "

"I'm taking you to the castle, whether you want to go or not. I'm going to do everything I can to find a cure for you and my father."

"Has anyone ever told you that you're very strong-willed?" said Rupert.

"I have to be to deal with stubborn people like you," Annie replied.

One of the guards came into the room, ducking his head when Annie looked his way. He had brought a small trunk and began to collect clothing and various things from around the room. Prince Rupert lay with his eyes closed, making Annie wonder if he'd fallen asleep. When the guard had filled the trunk, Annie gestured for him to set it by the door.

Rupert muttered, "I'm not going anywhere," without opening his eyes.

"We're leaving already?" Liam said as he walked into the room. "Oh, sorry," he whispered. "I didn't realize your uncle was asleep."

"He's not," said Annie. "He's just being stubborn. We're taking him back with us to the castle. He has the same illness as my father, only my uncle's has progressed much further. He's going back with us so we can get him and Father medical attention."

"And I'm going as well, right?" asked Clarence. "I'd hate to think I carried this bag all the way up those stairs for nothing."

Big Boy and Edda began to growl, a deep throaty sound that made the air vibrate. Clarence glanced at the dogs and backed into the corridor.

"Yes, you'll be going, too," said Annie. "I'm not leaving you in the fortress to take advantage of the commanding officer's absence. There's no telling what mischief you could get into then."

"I'm not getting out of this bed," said Rupert. "I can't stand on my own, let alone walk."

"Then we'll have to help you," said Annie. "Liam, if you can assist my uncle, I'm going to speak to the captain."

Liam nodded and started for the bed. He stopped to let Big Boy sniff his hand. When the dog wagged his tail, Liam petted his head and brushed past him to help Rupert. Satisfied that Liam could handle it, Annie returned to the corridor.

"Captain, we're leaving now," Annie told him. "My uncle is convinced that he's about to die, but I'm not going to let that happen."

"Very good," said the captain. "The prince is an excellent commanding officer. The men and I don't want to lose him. We'd be forever in your debt if you can indeed find a cure."

"Please don't pay any heed if he protests," Annie said. "He doesn't want to go."

"I'm sure you're right," the captain told her. "He finds it difficult to accept help from anyone."

"I'm not just anyone," said Annie. "This is one argument he's not going to win."

CHAPTER 4

EDDA AND BIG BOY went with them to the castle. Clarence had insisted that he stand as far from the dogs as possible, so he had placed himself on Liam's left side while Liam supported Prince Rupert on his right. Big Boy was propping his master up from the other side and Annie was sandwiched between the two troll dogs. Although they were huge, the dogs hadn't so much as stepped on her feet. She could see how her uncle could have come to depend on Big Boy.

The postcard worked as long as they were all touching, much like Annie's own anti-magic. As soon as they arrived at the castle, Clarence let go of Liam and started to walk away.

"Guards!" Liam called. "Please escort Prince Clarence into the great hall and don't let him leave. We have to decide what we're going to do with him while we're here."

When a group of guards came running, Annie called

two of them to her. "Please tell my mother that I've returned and need to speak to her right away," she told one man. Turning to the other, she added, "Run to the steward. Tell him that Prince Rupert has returned with us and needs the best accommodations that we can manage."

"Why don't I get the best accommodations?" Clarence whined as three guards hustled him off.

Prince Rupert sagged against Liam. "Sorry, but my legs really don't hold me now," Rupert told him. "I need to lie down."

Annie gestured to a big, burly guard, who picked up the ailing prince like he weighed nothing at all. The group hurried across the drawbridge, getting curious glances from everyone they met. Most people didn't recognize Rupert, who hadn't visited the castle in many years. He had grown up there, however, and some of the older castle residents recognized him. Word spread that the king's brother was back, and soon a crowd was following them into the great hall. They weren't there long before the steward had a room ready for him.

Annie was about to accompany her uncle upstairs when the guard she had sent to her mother returned. Queen Karolina was sitting by her window when Annie arrived. Her eyes grew wide when she saw Edda, but it wasn't until she noticed the look on her daughter's face that she motioned for her ladies-in-waiting to leave.

"What's wrong?" the queen asked Annie. "Did something happen in Dorinocco? Is King Montague all right?"

"The king is fine," Annie told her. "Liam doesn't want either his mother or his brother living in the castle once he becomes king, so we used one of the magic postcards to take Prince Clarence to the fortress at Delaroo Pass. We hoped to leave him there, but when I saw Uncle Rupert, we had to come straight here. We brought him with us. Mother, he has the same illness as Father, but he's in a much worse state. He claims to be dying and I believe him. Uncle Rupert says that their father died of the illness as well."

Queen Karolina's face had gone pale as she listened to Annie. Her hand was shaking when she put it to her cheek. "Isn't there something we can do to help them?" she asked.

"Uncle Rupert claims that the doctors tried everything when his father was dying, but there are new medicines now," said Annie. "I'm sure we'll find someone who can help Father and Rupert. I wanted to tell you what was going on before I got started. With your permission, I'm going to send for every doctor and herbalist in the kingdom. If there is a cure out there, we'll find it!"

"How will you get word out?" the queen asked.

"I'll see if I can get a few fairies to help," said Annie.

"I think I saw one or two flitting around the clover when we got here."

⁊

The doctors and herbalists began to arrive the next day. Some of the doctors rolled across the drawbridge in fancy carriages, while others arrived in creaking carts or on tired horses, having pushed their mounts to get there as quickly as they could. The local herbalist walked across the drawbridge carrying a heavy sack. A number of herbalists used magic to get there, arriving on a broom, in a washtub, or, like the woods witch Holly, in a shower of pine-scented sparkles.

"I'm worried about your father," Queen Karolina told Annie, "but he still refuses to let any more doctors near him. They should see Rupert now. His illness has progressed much further and his situation is dire.

"And I want the doctors to see him before the herbalists take their turns. I really think it will be a doctor who will have the cure."

"Then that's what we'll do." Annie turned to Ewan, who was waiting by the door. "Tell Horace to bring the doctors to Prince Rupert's chamber. Have him bring them in the order that they arrived."

The page nodded and hurried off. Annie watched him go, but she wasn't thinking about him at all. Her mother seemed to have more faith in the doctors than she did. Annie was glad that the herbalists were there.

Dr. Pencivale stepped into the room shortly after Queen Karolina and Annie. The moment he pulled a jar of leeches out of his bag, Annie had the guards escort him from the castle.

Dr. Hemshaw wanted to use a lancet to draw blood, saying, "We must remove the toxic humors!" He left just as quickly.

Dr. Learned, an older man who seemed quite sure of himself, made a great show of pouring a clear liquid into a silver chalice. "You must drink every drop," he told Rupert.

"What is it?" Rupert asked, eyeing the chalice with suspicion.

"Vinegar!" said the doctor. "It should do the trick!"

"I'm not drinking that!" the prince declared.

The doctor opened his bag again. "Then we'll try the mustard plasters. One for the chest and one for the back."

"No, you're not!" cried Rupert. "Get him away from me, Big Boy!"

The doctor gasped and dropped the bag when Big Boy stood up. "I thought that was a rug!" said the doctor, scurrying from the room.

"And he thought he was so smart!" Rupert grumbled.

Doctors Persnickety and Quarelle had ridden together, so Annie let them come in together as well. "We must shave his head and make him walk backward," said Dr. Persnickety.

"I disagree," said Dr. Quarelle. "The blue obviously goes from bottom to top. I believe he should stand on his head so that the blue will reverse itself and travel back up his legs and out through his toes."

"I disagree with both of you," said Annie. "My uncle can neither walk nor stand on his head, and your ideas are ridiculous. Thank you for coming, but we don't need your help today."

"We could try cupping," Dr. Quarelle told her as she hustled them from the room. "Raising blisters might pull out the toxins."

"Good-bye!" Annie said as she shut the door.

The last two doctors both believed that Rupert's body temperature was off. "He's blue because he's too cold," said Dr. Wartinger. "He needs to sit in a tub of hot water."

"He's too hot," Dr. Schmooze announced when it was his turn. "He's turning blue because his innards are cooking. He needs to sit in a tub of cold water."

"You're wrong," Annie told each of them. "You need to leave."

Because the herbalists all came with potions and tonics that could take some time to work, Annie gave them each one day.

The local herbalist, Frond, went first. "Here, drink this," she told Rupert, and poured an amber-colored tonic down his throat.

The tonic put him to sleep within minutes. He woke four hours later, shouting, "Help me!"

Big Boy started barking while the guards rushed to his side. "Did you see it? Is it still here?" asked Rupert.

"Is what still here, Uncle Rupert?" Annie asked him.

"The cat with flaming green eyes! It was as big as me!" the prince replied, his gaze darting around the room.

Frond started scribbling on a piece of parchment. "Produces sleep and wild dreams," she muttered as she wrote.

The blue had crept up his body an inch or so.

Calianth, a witch and herbalist from the southern tip of Treecrest, went next. "This salve will bring back his normal color," she said as she began to rub it on his skin.

It didn't. By the next day, the blue was halfway up his chest.

After a few more herbalists had tried to help without success, it was the turn of Holly, the woods witch. "I'm not sure what will work," Holly told Annie. "I've brought everything I could think of that might do some good, including some potions he can drink and salves we could put on him. To be honest, I've never seen or heard of an ailment like this and I doubt all those doctors and the other herbalists have, either."

"I'm sure you're right," said Annie. "Although I'm also sure that none of them would ever admit it. Do you have anything that you think might possibly work? Perhaps something that could slow the progress of the disease, even if it doesn't stop it?"

Holly shook her head. "The most I can do is help lessen the pain. Here," she said, pulling a small bottle from her bag. After tipping a little into Rupert's mouth, Holly stepped back and handed the bottle to Annie. "Give him just a few drops when he wakes up. No more for at least six hours after that."

Rupert's eyes seemed to glaze over. "Did I ever tell you that you look just like my niece, Annie?" he told Annie, and promptly fell asleep.

While the prince slept, Holly tried a dab of salve on one leg, and a different kind of salve on the other. When neither salve made any difference, the little witch looked at Annie and said, "There isn't a thing I can do. I'm so sorry."

"At least you were honest, unlike the rest of them," said Annie. "But I'm not giving up yet!"

శ

Although Annie wanted people to think that she was still hopeful, she was actually feeling miserable. No one seemed to be able to help her uncle or her father, and she had no idea what to do next. The "creeping blue," as they had started calling it, had almost reached her father's knees. He was beginning to find walking a challenge. Edda seemed to sense this and had taken up a post at his side, supporting him when he stood and walking beside him until he sat down again. Despite Edda's new dedication to the king, she still seemed to like Annie better than anyone and looked sad each time the princess walked out of the room. The only time the big dog ever left the king's side was when he was sleeping, something he seemed to do more often now. King Halbert was dozing in his bed when Annie went to check on him. Her mother was sitting by the window, embroidering, just as she'd been most of the day.

"I'll come back to see him later," Annie told her. "Would you like to join me for supper, or should I have something sent up?"

"I'll stay here a bit longer in case he wakes," said the queen. "I may still come to the hall; I need to stretch my legs."

"I hope you do," said Annie. "People have to see that you're all right." When Annie left the room, Edda stood and followed her down the stairs to the great hall.

People had grown used to seeing the huge dogs going to the kennel area to take care of business and walking to and from the royal brothers' bedchambers. Even so, when Annie came into the great hall with Edda at her side, people turned to stare. Annie was too caught up in her thoughts to notice, and Edda was interested only in Annie.

"Edda seems to be popular," Liam told Annie as she joined him on the dais.

Annie patted the great head resting on her lap. "I think the troll dogs give people something to think about other than Father's and Uncle Rupert's illness," said Annie. "Everyone needs a distraction at a time like this."

"I'm sure you're right," said Liam. "Speaking of distractions, here comes Clarence with his guard in tow."

"I'm glad the steward was able to find a suitable room for him," Annie replied.

"He isn't happy about being back in a tower," said Liam. "Unless he can sprout wings and fly, that's where he's staying until we decide what to do with him. It's nice of you to let him join us for supper, considering all he's tried to do to your family."

Annie shrugged. "He is your brother, although I have to admit he's not on my list of favorite people."

"Nor mine," said Liam. "Don't let it bother you when he gripes about the tower or the food or whatever he's thinking about at the moment. Mother raised him to expect more than he deserves."

Annie reached for her cup of cider and nodded to the girl who had just poured it. "I'm afraid Clarence's happiness is the least of my concerns. The creeping blue is moving up Father's legs, and he's not able to eat anything except soup and broth."

"That has to be the draftiest tower I've ever had the misfortune to be locked away in," Clarence said as he took a seat on the other side of Liam. "At least the tower at home had tapestries on the walls to block the wind coming through the cracks."

"Be glad you're not in the dungeon," Liam told him. "That's where I would have put you if I'd been King Halbert."

"If you were King Halbert, you'd be turning blue and counting the days until you die," said Clarence.

Liam scowled at his brother. "Be nice or I'll lock you in the dungeon myself," Liam said. "You know, Annie," he said, turning to face her. "I just thought of where we should take Clarence. I think the ice-dragon stronghold would be just the place for him. The dragons could stick him in that little room and freeze him like they froze those wizards."

"Don't tempt me," said Annie. "If he makes one more crack about my father, we may do just that."

"Dragons! Now I'm sure you're telling tall tales," said Clarence. "Everyone knows that dragons don't really exist."

Liam snorted and shook his head. "You may think whatever you want if it will make you happy. Oh, good! It looks as if your mother is going to join us for supper tonight, Annie."

Annie looked up and saw Queen Karolina coming through the door. Like Annie, the queen hadn't smiled in days. Although she was as beautiful as ever, she looked tired and worn.

"Your father is sleeping," the queen said as she sat

down beside Annie. "He may sleep for a while. This ill-ness is taking so much out of him."

"I'm sure we'll find something that will help him very soon," Annie told her. "There are so many marvels in this world that we're only just discovering. All we have to do is keep looking."

The servers were bringing platters of baked trout with onions and spit-turned venison coated in herbs when a guard came hurrying into the hall. "Your Highness," he said, looking from the queen to Annie. "Two people just arrived who claim to know Princess Annie and Prince Liam. They got here the same way you did, Princess. They weren't there, then suddenly they were."

"Really?" said Annie. "Did they give you their names?"

The guard nodded. "The lady says that she's Princess Millie. The young gentleman just called himself Audun."

"Bring them in!" Liam told him. "They're friends of ours."

While on their grand tour, one of the magic post-cards had taken Annie and Liam to a kingdom named Greater Greensward, where they'd met Millie and Audun. Millie was a human princess who could turn into a dragon, while Audun was a dragon who could turn into a human. The couple had helped Annie and Liam take care of the evil wizard who was following them, and ultimately helped them return home. At the end of their journey, Annie had given Millie a postcard so the human/dragon couple could visit Treecrest whenever they wished.

"They helped us through some difficulties on our grand tour," Annie explained to her mother. "I was hoping they'd come visit someday. I just didn't expect them so soon."

Annie and Liam waited expectantly while the guard hurried from the hall. A few minutes later, the guard reappeared with Millie and Audun.

"Huh," said Clarence as the two newcomers approached the dais. "Your friend Millie is pretty, but she's not nearly as beautiful as most princesses."

"That's because she comes from a place where royalty isn't made beautiful through magic," said Annie. "Millie is naturally beautiful, just as Audun is naturally handsome."

Queen Karolina leaned toward her daughter and whispered, "I've never seen hair that color on such a young man before. Is it silver or white?"

"Silvery white, I think," said Annie. "I believe it's not uncommon in his family."

"I've never heard of such a thing!" Clarence declared. "Where is there a kingdom so backward that royalty doesn't get important magical christening gifts?"

"Very far away," Annie told him. "And I don't think they're at all backward or that beauty is that important."

"Be polite to our friends or I'll have you escorted back to the tower," Liam told his brother.

"You're always threatening me!" Clarence said, sitting back in his seat and scowling.

Edda sat up and sniffed the air as the new arrivals approached. She seemed to find their scent interesting, but not at all threatening. Satisfied, she lay down again, grunting as she returned her head to Annie's lap.

"Millie, Audun, how wonderful that you've come to see us!" Annie said as her friends drew closer. "Mother, I'd like you to meet Princess Millie and her husband, Prince Audun."

Audun raised an eyebrow at being called a prince, but Millie just smiled and bowed to the queen. "I'm delighted to meet Annie's mother," said Millie. "Audun and I like your daughter very much."

The queen almost smiled when she said, "So do I. And I'm delighted to meet some of Annie's friends. I don't know how you helped her, but I must thank you for whatever you did. Ah, I see that Ewan has come to get me. I told him to let me know when King Halbert awakes. Excuse me for leaving just as you arrived, Millie, but my husband is quite ill."

"I'm so sorry to hear that!" Millie told her.

"Edda, are you coming with me?" the queen asked the dog. "I know she'd rather stay with you, Annie, but your father finds her presence comforting."

"That's all right," said Annie. "I'll get her back when I come up to say good night."

Edda stood and turned mournful eyes on Annie. "Be

a good girl and help my father," Annie told her. "I'll see you very soon."

The dog followed the queen from the room, stopping in the doorway once, as if to see if Annie had changed her mind.

"That dog really loves you," Millie said to Annie as they both watched the dog leave. "Have you had her a long time?"

Annie shook her head. "Just a few days, although I'm already fond of her, too."

"Dogs and horses don't usually like me," said Millie. "I've never learned to ride because of it, and my father's dogs avoid me as if I carried the plague. It's nice to see a dog that doesn't act that way."

"Edda is a very discerning dog. She doesn't like trolls or certain people," Annie said, glancing at Clarence.

"Tell me, what's wrong with your father?" asked Millie. "You didn't mention that he was ill when we saw you last."

"He wasn't then," said Annie. "He didn't show signs of it until after we'd returned. We call it the creeping blue, but I'm sure it has some other name. It started when his feet turned blue and he lost his appetite. The blue is creeping up his legs now and walking has become difficult. My uncle has it as well, but his illness is much further along. He's in pain, too, although my father hasn't reached that point yet. We're afraid my uncle doesn't have much longer to live. We've had all the doctors and

47

herbalists in the kingdom out to see him, but none of them were able to help. Have you ever heard of anything like it? Please tell me you know how to cure it!"

Millie's eyes looked sad when she shook her head. "I'm sorry, but I've never heard of a disease like that."

"We're actually on our way to find a doctor ourselves," said Audun. "I'm worried about Millie's health. Our baby will be the first one born to an ice dragon and a—"

"Did he say 'ice dragon'?" asked Clarence, leaning forward in his seat.

"Don't be ridiculous!" said Annie. "You said yourself that dragons aren't real. He said 'a nice maiden.' Didn't you, Audun?"

"Uh, yes, exactly!" Audun declared. "I was going to say, our baby will be the first one born to a nice maiden and a member of my family. We're all scoundrels, you see."

"Even the women?" asked Clarence.

"Especially the women!" replied Audun. "You should see my grandmother argue with the king!"

"I'm sorry I didn't introduce you," Liam told Audun. "This is my brother, Prince Clarence."

"It's nice to meet you," said Audun.

"You're not well?" Annie asked Millie in a quiet voice.

"I wouldn't say that exactly," her friend replied. "It's just that my stomach has been bothering me a lot."

"An old witch named Mudine told us about an excellent witch doctor named Ting-Tang," added Audun. "She said that he lives in a place called Skull Cove, on the other side of the world from Greater Greensward. You're on the other side of the world, so Millie and I thought that Skull Cove might be near you and Liam. We were hoping that someone here could tell us how to get there."

"Do you think he might be able to help my father?" Annie asked.

"I should think that he could if anyone could," Millie told her. "Mudine said he can do amazing things and is the best doctor she's ever met."

"I've never heard of Skull Cove," said Annie.

"Neither have I," Liam told them.

"Of course no one thinks to ask me," Clarence declared. "And I'm the only one here who actually went to sea."

"Do you know where Skull Cove is, Clarence?" asked Audun.

"I do, indeed," Clarence replied, looking smug. "I could take you there if you'd like."

"That would be wonderful!" Millie exclaimed.

"Or you could give us directions and we could take our friends there," Liam told Clarence.

"That's not happening," Clarence replied. "I don't know the names of the landmarks, but I would recognize them when I saw them. I have to go with you if you want my help."

"Why am I not surprised?" Annie murmured to herself.

"What did you say?" asked Clarence.

"I said that it looks as if we're all going," said Annie. "I'll tell Mother that we'll be leaving in the morning."

CHAPTER 5

AFTER CLARENCE RETURNED to the tower, the two couples pored over maps, trying to find Skull Cove. As far as they could tell, it wasn't on any of King Halbert's maps, nor could they find any mention of it in his books. Because Clarence had refused to tell them even as much as the direction they'd be heading, all they knew was that they would have to travel by sea.

"Kenless is the closest large port where we can hire a ship," said Liam. "If we leave before dawn tomorrow, we should be able to get there before nightfall. I'll send some men ahead to see if they can book a ship for us."

"Why do we need a ship?" asked Audun. "Can't we just fly there? Millie and I carried you to the ice-dragon stronghold on our backs without any problem."

"Oh, no!" said Annie. "You can't let anyone see that you're dragons. You can't even talk about dragons when someone might hear you. There are no fire-breathing or ice dragons in our part of the world, so people are convinced that they don't exist. The closest creatures we have to dragons are the wyverns in eastern Treecrest. Everyone is terrified of them and with good reason. The wyverns are nasty creatures that kill anyone passing through their territory. People call them dragons because they don't know any better."

"I get it now! That's why you pretended I wasn't talking about dragons at supper," said Audun.

Annie nodded. "I don't want anyone trying to shoot you down with arrows or run you through with a pike. People who are afraid of something they don't understand can do truly horrible things."

"Your brother included?" Audun asked Liam.

"Especially Clarence!" said Liam. "I think he denies the existence of dragons so strongly because he's afraid of them. When we were young, we had a nursemaid who told us stories about fierce dragons and brave knights. I enjoyed the stories, but they gave Clarence nightmares."

"Then we won't let him know that we can turn into dragons," said Millie. "I've been wondering why your brother is under guard. Are you protecting him from something?"

"We're just trying to keep him from running off or doing something he shouldn't," said Liam. "Clarence isn't known for making the best decisions. He and my mother tried to take over Treecrest. Then he sided with a nasty wizard and tried to take over Dorinocco. Annie and I are looking for a place where we can leave him and he can't cause any trouble."

"You mean you want to banish him," said Audun.

"Exactly!" Liam replied.

ॐ

When the couples finally said good night and went their separate ways, Annie and Liam headed to her father's chamber. They found her mother still there, fussing over the king as she tried to get him to drink some broth.

"We've come to say good-bye," Annie told them. "Millie and Audun say there's a doctor at a place called Skull Cove who might be able to help you, Father. We're leaving at the first change of the guard."

"Do you have to go so early?" asked her mother.

"I'd leave now if I could, but we need to get some rest and pack our things. The sooner we get started, the sooner we'll be back with medicine for Father and Uncle Rupert."

"I don't know what we'd do without you, Annie," her father said, looking more tired and vulnerable than she'd ever seen him. "Take good care of her, Liam. I was a fool not to recognize how precious she was all those years."

Annie left before the tears welling up in her eyes showed just how upset she felt. Her parents had only recently started treating her like family, and now this! The trip to the witch doctor had to work! It just had to!

୨୭

They left the next day in the small hours of the morning. Although it had been hard to leave her parents the night before, it was almost as hard to leave Edda, whose sad eyes made Annie feel guilty as she descended the steps into the courtyard. She knew that the dog would dedicate herself to the king in Annie's absence, but Annie couldn't help but feel that she was abandoning a dear friend.

They were taking a carriage because neither Millie nor Audun was able to ride a horse. Even the horses pulling the carriage were afraid of them. Annie had to distract the horses with sweet-smelling hay while her friends took their seats. The horses still acted uneasy, stomping their feet and pinning their ears back.

When Clarence climbed into the carriage, he was already grumbling. "I don't know why one of you couldn't have bothered to tell me that we were leaving so early! It's a good thing I never unpacked my bag. Isn't keeping a man from getting his sleep some kind of torture? That old guard, Horace I think his name was, pulled me out of bed by my foot! I'm a prince! No one does that to a prince! I was sound asleep having a very nice dream, too. The way you're treating me is inhuman!"

"You can sleep in the carriage," Annie said as she sat

down beside him. "The ship, too, unless, of course, Skull Cove is close by."

"I know what you're up to," said Clarence. "I'm not telling you anything about the cove's location. You'll just have to wait and see."

"Is everything all right in here?" Liam said, sticking his head in the door. "Ah, good, you're all settled in."

"You're not getting in here, too, are you?" asked Clarence.

Liam shook his head. "Not today. I'll be riding Hunter, but I'll be right outside if anyone needs me."

"Why do you get to ride a horse while I have to sit in this dark, smelly carriage where I can't even stretch my legs?" Clarence asked his brother.

"Because there isn't room for me in there, and if you rode a horse, you'd take off and we'd never see you again when we actually need your help," Liam told him. "Be nice to everyone or you'll answer to me."

Clarence started to grumble again, but no one paid him any attention.

"I'll see you soon, my love," Liam said, leaning in to give Annie a kiss.

He was closing the door when Clarence turned to Audun. "What about you? Why are you sitting in a stuffy carriage instead of riding a horse and enjoying the fresh air?"

"Because he's being a gentleman and keeping me company," said Millie.

"That's a lousy reason," Clarence said, but he closed his eyes and didn't say anything more.

It was still dark out as they rattled across the drawbridge; the guards who had lowered it yawned as they waved to their friends in the mounted escort. Leaving the field that fronted the castle, the carriage rumbled south through the forest, where even the birds were asleep. Lanterns swung from the front of the carriage, lighting their way. Millie was soon dozing, holding Audun's hand, but Annie was wide-awake, despite having had only a few hours' sleep. She was worried about her father and uncle and how they might fare in her absence.

And then there was the voyage itself. Although she and Liam had originally planned to take a sea voyage for their grand tour, now that she was actually going on one, she began to get uneasy. She had never set foot on a ship before, but she had flown over the ocean on dragon back. Some of the strange creatures she had spotted below them had looked awfully frightening. Mostly, however, she was worried about the success of the trip, knowing that this might be the last chance to save her father's and uncle's lives.

An extra-large bump in the road startled Annie from her reverie. She peered out the carriage window, wishing she knew where they were. When Liam rode up, she talked to him for a few minutes. Otherwise, there was nothing to look at but the trees.

They stopped at noon to water the horses and let the passengers out to walk around. Liam dug a packet of food from his saddlebag and the others joined him in the shade of a tree. He had brought dried fish for the dragons, although Clarence took a piece as well. Fruit, bread, and sausage made up the rest of their meal.

Annie was nibbling grapes when a small cloud of fairies appeared, clustering around her. "Princess! You came to see us!" said a fairy wearing a bluebell cap.

"We had so much fun at your wedding!" declared the fairy with a fluffy dandelion puff on her head.

A fairy dressed in a rose-petal gown came to hover right in front of Annie. "It was the most beautiful wedding ever! We brought some of the flowers."

The fairy wearing violets pushed her friend aside. "Every one of us helped, some more than others," she said, glancing at the fairy covered in moss.

"I helped, too!" the mossy fairy said, almost bumping into Clarence in her hurry to correct her friend.

Clarence was digging through the remains of the food and not really paying attention to the fairies. When the moss-covered fairy came too close, Clarence waved his hand in the air as if brushing away a fly. He hit the fairy, sending her spinning into her friends.

"Help!" the fairy shrieked.

"You big bully!" cried the rose-petal fairy. "How dare you hit Moss!"

"Wait!" Annie cried as the fairy raised her wand.

"Please don't use your magic on him. He's just a clumsy oaf who hit Moss by mistake. I'm sure he's sorry. Aren't you, Clarence?"

Clarence's eyes crossed when he looked at the angry fairy who had flown close enough to tap him with her wand. "Uh, yeah. Sorry!" he said, leaning back.

The fairy still looked as if she was going to tap Clarence, but when she glanced at Annie, her expression softened. "I'll let it go this time because you asked, Princess. But if this fool ever assaults one of my friends again, I'll turn him into a ... worm!"

"No! A gnat!" cried Moss.

"A snail!" shouted another fairy.

"A stinkbug!" "A spider mite!" "A weevil!" suggested some others.

"Clarence, I think you should get back in the carriage before someone gets a little carried away," said Annie.

Clarence got to his feet and backed off. "I'll finish my lunch in there." Leaning down, he snatched up the last pieces of food, then hurried back to the carriage.

Annie spent the next few minutes calming the fairies. They were especially happy when she invited them to come to the coronation in Dorinocco, although she told them she wasn't sure of the date yet.

"Are the fairies here always that prickly?" Millie asked when Annie finally climbed into the carriage.

"They are," Annie told her. "You have to be careful

what you say and do around them. When they thought we hadn't invited them to our wedding, they used their magic to ruin it. Clarence, you need to keep in mind that fairies may be small, but they can destroy your life with their magic."

"Huh," he grunted, acting as if he didn't care, but she thought his face was a little paler than usual.

The carriage had rumbled a few more miles down the road when Liam rode up to the window. "Did I hear you right? Did you invite the fairies to the coronation?"

Annie nodded. "I think we're going to have to invite the fairies to all our big events," she told him. "It's going to be the only way to stay on their good side."

"Do you mean all the fairies from Treecrest and Dorinocco?" asked Liam.

"Every one!" Annie replied, laughing when she saw the look on his face.

ॐ

They stopped to water the horses at a stream a few hours later. Clarence jumped out of the carriage as soon as a guard opened the door. He was inching away from the group when Annie noticed. "You might want to tell the guards to keep a better watch over your brother. He looks as if he's going to try to sneak away."

Liam glanced at Clarence and nodded. "Good idea," he said. "I don't want to have to scour the woods looking for him when time is so important. Guards! Two of you have to watch my brother every time he steps out of the carriage. He looks as if he's about to go for a stroll."

The guards all turned toward Clarence. Two of them took up posts on either side of him and hustled him back to the carriage. He was scowling when they forced him inside.

It was late afternoon when they stopped again. The guards were extra vigilant around Clarence, following him even when he went to use the bushes. This annoyed him so much that he stomped back, refusing the water that Annie offered to him. "What do they think I'm going to do, run off into the trees and meet up with my cronies who just happen to be waiting here in the middle of nowhere? Can't a man have a little privacy?"

"People we trust get privacy," Liam told him. "You don't deserve our trust."

They left the forest soon after that. A narrow bridge took them over the River Gargle and into the kingdom of Shimshee. Only a few miles from Kenless, one of the horses threw a shoe. They stopped in the closest town and were fortunate enough to find a blacksmith. "We might as well have supper while we're here," Liam told Annie through the window when he spotted an inn across the street.

"I hope they have something other than dried fish and sausage. There wasn't enough sausage and the fish was oily. I could scarcely finish mine," said Clarence.

Annie glanced at Millie and Audun. Clarence had taken part of their food and was complaining about it. They were probably hungrier than he was, but hadn't said a word about it. The more she got to know Millie and Audun, the more she liked them.

The inn was nearly full when they entered, but the innkeeper seemed happy to move some tables and chairs around when he saw the guards' livery. Millie and Audun were delighted with the fresh salmon served at the inn, and even Annie found it too tempting to turn down. They had almost finished their meal when a guard walked into the inn, looking for them. "The blacksmith replaced the shoe, Your Highness," he told Liam. "We're ready to go when you are."

Everyone else stood up, but Clarence just helped himself to more bread. "You don't want me to waste away, do you?" he asked when he saw everyone looking at him.

Liam sighed and stepped outside with the guard. When he came back in, Clarence was finally ready to go. They were walking out the door when Liam took Annie aside. "I told you that I sent some men ahead to Kenless to locate a ship. We'll board as soon as we reach the city. It will be faster and we're less likely to lose Clarence that way."

"Good thinking," said Annie. When he went off to tell the others, Annie noticed that Clarence was talking to a barmaid while his guards listened to Liam. He handed the young woman something, which she looked at and pocketed before hurrying away. Annie assumed that Clarence had ordered food for the road.

When they were finally climbing into the carriage again, Clarence held back. "What is your brother doing now?" Annie asked Liam.

"I don't know!" Liam said, sounding irritated. "Guards, I think my brother needs to get in the carriage first."

Clarence balked, but got in the carriage when the guards made him. After everyone else had piled in, they started to drive away. "Hey!" a man shouted.

Annie looked out the window when the carriage stopped. A hostler leading a horse ducked his head in respect before walking up to Liam just outside Annie's window. "What should I do with the horse?" the man asked.

"What are you talking about?" asked Liam.

"The horse that man just bought," the hostler said, holding up some coins. "He gave Betha money to buy a horse and bring it to him here. Doesn't he want the horse?"

Liam laughed and shook his head. "Not anymore!"

The man looked confused. "Then what should I do with it?"

"Keep it!" said Liam, and waved for the carriage to go on.

Annie turned to look at Clarence. "You never give up, do you?"

"I don't know what you're talking about," he said. Settling back in his seat, he closed his eyes and pretended to go to sleep.

Annie sighed and shook her head. Traveling with Clarence made everything a challenge.

CHAPTER 6

ANNIE COULD SMELL the ocean before she could see it. A breeze carried the tang of the salt air over the hills that surrounded Kenless, making her sit up in her seat and peer out the window. Her anticipation grew as they drew closer, and it seemed to take forever for the carriage to go up and over the last hill.

It was dusk when they reached the wall surrounding Kenless. The men that Liam had sent ahead were waiting at the gate.

"We've booked a ship, Your Highness," one of the men told Liam. "We can board the *Sallie Mae* at any time, but Prince Digby found out that you were coming to town and wants to see you and Princess Annie."

Liam grimaced. "I was hoping to leave as soon as possible. Ah, well, it's only common courtesy to see him when we're in his city. Are those men here to escort us to the castle?"

When Liam indicated a group of men in the livery of Shimshee's royal family, the guard replied, "They're waiting for you, but not to take you to the castle. Prince Digby is in the Rusty Nail. It's that tavern on the corner."

"It looks fairly disreputable," said Liam. "I'm not sure I want to take Princess Annie there."

"That's the thing, Your Highness," said the guard. "Prince Digby insisted that Annie has to come see him, too."

"I'll go if it will get us to the ship faster," Annie told Liam.

"Are you on good terms with this Digby?" asked Audun. "Could this be some sort of trap?"

"I wouldn't call our relationship good," said Annie. "We never did like each other and we still don't. I suppose it didn't help that he used to be engaged to my sister, but I brought another prince named Beldegard to see her and he turned out to be her true love. And then I helped my friend Snow White find her true love, and that wasn't Digby, either."

"Do you think he might mean you harm?" Millie asked.

Annie shrugged. "I doubt it, although I suppose it's possible."

"Then we're going, too," Millie told her.

When Liam nodded, the carriage rolled through the gates and stopped in front of the tavern. Annie got out with Millie and Audun close behind. Clarence scrambled out after them and was the first to enter the tavern.

"Help me!" he cried when he saw Digby seated at a table. "I'm being abducted!"

"Be quiet, Clarence," said Liam. "No one is abducting you. I'm banishing you. There's a big difference. Guard, please escort my brother back to the carriage. You may gag him if you have to, but keep him quiet."

When a guard laid his hand on Clarence's shoulder, the prince shrugged him off and stepped aside, tripping over the leg of a chair so he landed at the innkeeper's feet. The innkeeper gave him a hand up. Annie could have sworn she saw a look pass between them, and thought they held on to each other just a little too long. Annie was about to say something, but then Clarence turned and let the guards hustle him to the carriage without complaint.

"Liam! Annie! I was surprised to hear that you were back from your grand tour so soon," Digby said, raising a tankard to them. "Is married life really that bad?"

"It looks as if he's been drinking for a while," Liam whispered to Annie.

Annie nodded and took Liam's hand. "Married life is lovely," she told Digby.

Prince Digby raised the tankard to his lips and chugged the contents. Slamming it on the table, he wiped his mouth with the back of his hand and said,

"Good to hear it! That's why I wanted to see you. Marriage! I want a wife and I want you to help me."

"I don't understand," said Annie. "What do you expect me to do?"

"Find me the love of my life!" said Digby as a barmaid filled his tankard again. "My father ordered me to get married and settle down, but so far no woman will have me."

"I don't know how I'd—" Annie began.

"You helped Gwendolyn and Snow White. It's time you did the same for me!" Digby said. He leaned toward the table as he reached for his tankard. Instead of picking it up, however, he laid his arm on the sticky tabletop, and then laid his head on his arm. A moment later, he began to snore.

"That was faster than I was afraid it might be," Liam said, ushering his wife and friends out of the tavern.

"I've never seen a prince act that way before," Millie said as she took her seat in the carriage. "Do princes in this part of the world do that kind of thing often?"

"Only Digby, as far as I know," said Annie.

"What do you mean by 'this part of the world'?" asked Clarence.

"Why aren't you gagged?" Audun asked him.

"Because I promised to keep my mouth shut, and a guard kept a dagger at my throat until you came out, that's why," said Clarence. "Now you answer my question.

What do you mean by 'this part of the world'? Where are you from exactly?"

"A kingdom called Greater Greensward," Millie said as the carriage started to move. "It's so far away that I'm sure you've never heard of it."

"Huh," Clarence said as he leaned back in his seat. "I bet you just made that name up!"

༄

The sun started to set as they passed through the warren of narrow streets on their way to the docks. It was nearly dark when they left the carriage and climbed up the ramp to the deck of the *Sallie Mae*. The first thing Annie noticed was the scent of freshly cut wood, turpentine, and tar. When she tilted her head back to look up, she thought that the masts seemed to disappear into the night sky, and that the furled sails were so white, they almost seemed to glow. Although it was too dark for her to see much else, she guessed that the ship was fairly new; she couldn't wait to get a better look at it in the morning.

While Liam and Clarence talked to the captain, Annie, Millie, and Audun followed a young sailor to their cabins. He opened a door for Millie and Audun first, ushering them into a snug cabin with a bunk bed.

"Good night," Millie said, yawning. "I'm going straight to bed. I'm so tired, I can barely keep my eyes open."

"But you slept all day in the carriage," said her husband.

"I know, and it was exhausting!" Millie said with a laugh. "Any idea when we'll set sail?"

"The captain said we'd go at first light," Annie told her. "Have you ever been on a ship before?"

Millie shook her head. "Never! I'm so excited!" she said, and yawned again.

"Good night!" Annie told her friends, and turned to follow the sailor.

Her cabin was just a few more doors down a short corridor. The sailor opened the door and stepped aside to let her go in first. Two of Liam's guards followed her into the cabin, bringing the baggage that she and Liam had packed. It was a large cabin with a big bed on one side and a desk on the other. Annie hadn't expected it to be so nice, but then she heard the sailor tell the guards, "The captain's never given up his cabin for anyone before, but then, this is the first time we've had royalty on board."

Minutes after the sailor and the guards left, Liam stepped into the cabin. He looked around, saying, "It will do. I wanted to tell you that our guards won't be traveling with us. The captain says that there isn't room on the ship, so they'll wait for our return here in Kenless."

Annie shrugged. "We've traveled without guards before. Is everything settled with the captain? Did Clarence tell him where to go?"

"They were looking at charts when I left them. I think that—"

There was a knock on the door and a tentative voice called, "Your Highness?"

"Yes, what is it?" Liam called back.

"Pardon me, Your Highness," the sailor replied. "Captain Riley respectfully requests your presence on deck."

Liam sighed. "This is turning into a very long day. I'll be right back, my darling," he said, and gave Annie a quick kiss.

He was heading toward the door when she announced, "I'm going with you," and hurried after him.

Annie and Liam found the captain on deck, arguing with Clarence. "Prince Clarence isn't cooperating," the captain said when he saw them. "You said that he would tell me where we're going, but he refuses to tell me much of anything. We can't leave port until I know which heading to take."

"I told you to head west," Clarence declared. "I'll tell you when to change course. I'm going to bed. I'll see you all in the morning. Not too early, though. I need my rest."

The captain shook his head as Clarence started for the stairs. "I've never taken my ship anywhere that I couldn't find on a chart before we set sail. The prince mentioned a place called Skull Cove, but I can't find it on any of my charts or maps. Are you sure this place exists?"

"I sincerely hope so," said Annie. "The lives of my father and my uncle depend on it."

When Annie woke, she realized that the movement of the ship was different than it had been the night before. It wasn't just rolling with the waves now; it was actually moving forward. Seeing that Liam had already left the cabin, she washed and got dressed, then hurried after him. She found him standing with Audun by the railing, watching the passing coastline as they headed south-west across the sea.

"Oh, good, you're up!" Liam said when he saw her. "I tried not to disturb you when I saw you sleeping so peacefully."

Annie smiled and kissed him. "That was the first good night's rest I've gotten since we brought Rupert back from the fortress. Thank you for letting me sleep. How is Millie this morning?" she asked Audun.

"Not so good," Audun told her. "Even before we left port, the rocking of the ship was already upsetting her stomach. I don't think she got any sleep last night."

"Perhaps I should go see her," said Annie.

Audun shook his head. "The last thing she wants right now is company. She kicked me out of the cabin at dawn, telling me that if she was going to be miserable, she wanted to do it alone."

"All right," said Annie. "If you're sure that's what she wants."

Liam pointed at the shoreline they were passing. "Look, Annie, those are the hills of Corealis. We should be passing Wryden soon."

71

"We move much faster by sea than we ever have by horseback," Annie remarked.

"Or by carriage," Clarence said as he joined them. "We're also going faster than usual because we have the wind behind us. I wasn't expecting that."

Annie thought he looked worried, as if there was something wrong with going fast.

The captain was walking toward them, also wearing a worried look. "Prince Clarence, may I ask when I can expect more directions?"

"I can't give you any until I see certain landmarks," Clarence told him. "But I can say that it won't be today."

Liam's hand was resting on the railing. Annie placed her hand on top of his and moved closer to his side. The fresh salt air and the way the ship was racing through the waves were exhilarating. Glancing up at the billowing sails, she suddenly understood why some people loved sailing. This was so much better than traveling by carriage! Part of her was in a hurry to reach Skull Cove and return to her father and uncle with medicine, but another part of her wished that this day and this trip would never end.

They sailed that whole day and well into the next with the wind behind them and the sun shining overhead. Millie stayed in her cabin, but the others spent most of their time on deck. When Annie spotted a group of large fishlike creatures with long, rounded snouts and friendly eyes, a passing sailor told her that they were called porpoises and were friends to sailors everywhere. Annie watched them jump out of the water as if they were playing and was disappointed when they moved on.

Although the captain asked Clarence about directions throughout the day, it wasn't until they spotted an island in the distance that Clarence really began to look around. The island didn't appear to be that far off, but Annie thought it seemed to take forever to reach it. As they drew closer, they were able to make out more of its features. Sheer cliffs that denied access to passing ships were the home of countless squawking, swooping birds. In the center of the island, a large rocky outcropping jutted up from a forest of scrubby trees.

Clarence became more animated now, gazing off across the ocean as if he expected to see something other than rolling waves. When he had turned completely around, apparently without seeing whatever it was he'd been hoping to find, he finally went to see Captain Riley.

"Turn south now," he told the captain, then went back to gazing into the distance.

The captain turned the ship south, rounding the island. They sailed in that direction for a few hours while Clarence became increasingly agitated. When he finally told the captain to head east, Liam went to talk to his brother.

"I thought you said you knew where you were going," said Liam.

"I do!" Clarence declared. "I'm looking for landmarks. You'll just have to trust me."

Liam laughed. "That's never going to happen! If you don't want to tell me what to look for, why don't you tell the captain? Then you can both try to find these landmarks."

"And if I tell him, what's to keep you from tossing me overboard?" Clarence asked him. "As long as you need me, I'll have safe passage. I'm not doing anything to jeopardize that."

"I would never toss him over," Liam told Annie when he returned to her side. "But I bet he'd toss us all over if he got the chance. I can't believe we're depending on him for anything, let alone directions."

"It's not like we had a choice," said Annie. "We'll just have to keep an eye on him."

As the day grew hotter, Annie began to worry about Millie. She knew that the cabins were stuffy with no windows that opened, which would only make her friend feel worse. Fetching a mug of cider from the galley, she made her way down to the cabin and found Millie still lying in her bunk.

"How are you feeling?" asked Annie.

Millie glanced up. "Not very well," she said in a faint voice.

Annie offered her the mug. "Would cider help?"

Groaning, Millie shook her head. "I can't keep anything down. Is Audun all right?"

"He's fine," said Annie. "He and Liam are playing a

game of cards on deck. Is there anything that I can get for you that might help?"

"No, thank you," Millie told her. "I'll probably be better in a day or two when the water isn't so rough."

"It isn't rough now," Annie told her.

Millie just moaned.

When Annie went back on deck, she found Liam and Audun drinking from tankards. "This is really good," Liam told her. "You should try it."

"What is that?" Annie asked.

"Juice they had in the galley," Audun told her. "Clarence was drinking some and he highly recommended it."

"Here, take a sip," said Liam. "If you like it, I'll get you your own."

Annie took the tankard from him. She had already taken a sip when she noticed a very faint sound. It took her a moment to tell that it was coming from the drink. "Don't drink it!" she told Liam and Audun. "There's a magic potion in the drink! I can hear it!"

"What kind of potion?" Audun asked, frowning.

"I'm not sure, but my guess is a sleeping potion," she said as Liam slumped to the deck, yawning.

"He should lie down the rest of the way," Audun said, easing him onto the wood planking.

Liam was asleep and snoring loudly when Annie knelt down beside him and touched his chest. He stirred and half opened his eyes. "What happened?" he murmured.

"Your brother gave you a sleeping potion," Annie told him.

"I'm going to check on Millie," announced Audun. "Clarence said he'd found her a drink that would make her feel better."

"I don't think you need to worry," said Annie. "The magic didn't work on either of us. Clarence must have brought the potion with him. Any magic he has wouldn't affect me. And you and Millie are dragons, so it wouldn't affect you, either."

"Maybe so," said Audun, "but if Clarence will put his own brother to sleep, I don't want him going anywhere near my wife!"

While Audun hurried to his cabin to see Millie, Annie got to her feet. Liam fell asleep again as soon as she stopped touching him. "I'll be right back, my love," she assured her sleeping husband. "I need to do something about that juice. We don't want the captain or his crew falling asleep when no one else knows how to sail the ship!"

It took Annie only a few minutes to reach the galley and pour out the rest of the potion-laced juice. She was back on deck when Audun came storming up the stairs. "Is Millie all right?" she asked.

Audun scowled. "Clarence convinced her that the juice would settle her stomach. It didn't, though; it just made her sick all over again. Where is that little weasel? I'm going to throttle him."

"I have no idea," Annie said as she sat down beside Liam. "But before you throttle him, please ask how long this sleeping potion is supposed to last. I'll hold Liam's hand all day if I have to, but it would be nice to know that won't be necessary."

૨✦

It was dark by the time the potion wore off. Audun had carried Liam to the cabin, so he had no idea how he had gotten there. "What's going on?" Liam asked again.

"I told you before; your brother put a sleeping potion in that juice. It didn't affect anyone but you and one crew member who drank some before I poured it out. Clarence denied it at first, but Audun was able to make him confess. He never did say why he did it, though."

"That rat!" Liam said, swinging his legs over the side of the bed. "When I get my hands on him, I'll—"

"He locked himself in his cabin," said Annie. "Short of breaking down the door, you're not going to be able to talk to him tonight, and I doubt the captain would appreciate any door breaking on his ship."

"Then I'll speak to him in the morning," Liam said as he lay back down. "Maybe I will toss him overboard, at least long enough to teach him a lesson. Wow! My head feels very strange."

"Magic potions will do that to you," said Annie. "At least that's what I've been told."

CHAPTER 7

ALTHOUGH ANNIE WOKE UP early the next day, Liam had already left the cabin. After using the washbasin and changing her clothes, Annie went to the door and found that it wouldn't open. When jiggling the door latch didn't work, she tried to find a way to open the door, but it was definitely locked from the outside. "I'm locked in!" she called, pounding on the door. "Can somebody help me?"

Annie staggered when the ship listed to the side. They were changing course. Clarence must have seen another landmark. She was pounding on the door again when she heard a bang and a crash. A moment later, someone undid the lock. When her door swung open, Audun was there. Annie could still smell the dragon scent as if he had just changed back.

"Are you all right?" he asked.

"I'm fine," said Annie. "Why was my door locked?"

"I have no idea, but mine was, too. I intend to find out why and who did it," said Audun. "Millie is feeling better today. I was going to take her up on deck when I discovered that someone had locked us in. I'm afraid we'll have to pay the captain for the door. I broke it down when I felt the ship change direction."

"It must have been Clarence again," Annie said.

"That's what Millie and I think," Audun replied as she followed him out the door. "I guess my little talk with him yesterday wasn't as effective as I'd hoped. I told him I'd rip his head off if he ever again did anything that could hurt my wife. I think locking her in when she needs fresh air qualifies."

Millie was waiting just inside the remains of the door when they reached the cabin. "This trip hasn't been at all what I expected," she said, taking Audun's hand as she stepped over the splintered wood. "I've heard about seasickness, but I never imagined it could be so awful. And Audun told me that Clarence used magic on everyone! I wonder what he's up to."

"I hope Liam is all right," said Annie. "He was gone when I woke up."

"I heard raised voices earlier," Audun told her. "I think he was arguing with Clarence."

Annie and Millie followed him up the steps. When they reached the deck, Annie stopped to look around.

Something was different, but she couldn't tell what until she noticed that the sun was straight ahead and the island was still on their left.

"We're headed back the way we came," said Annie. "Do you suppose Clarence is lost?"

"There's Liam. He looks fine to me," Millie told her. "It looks like he and Clarence are talking to the captain."

Annie and her friends hurried over, full of questions. Clarence seemed surprised to see them, but both Liam and Captain Riley wore dazed expressions.

"Who locked us in the cabins?" demanded Audun. "Clarence, was it you?"

"Why would I do that?" Clarence said, trying to look innocent without much success.

"That's exactly what I want to know," Audun said, his voice nearly a growl.

"Why did we change direction?" Annie asked Liam. "Did Clarence see the landmark he was trying to find?"

"We didn't change direction, did we?" Liam asked the captain.

Captain Riley looked just as confused, even though he was standing with his hand on the helm.

"What's that smell?" Millie asked, sniffing the air. "Do you smell that, Audun?"

Her husband inhaled and nodded. "It's coming from over here."

He followed his nose to Clarence. The prince's hand went to his pocket as if to make sure that something was tucked inside. Clarence tried to fend off Audun, but dragons are stronger than humans, even when in human form. "What is this?" Audun said as he pulled a stoppered vial out of Clarence's pocket.

"I don't know," said Clarence. "I've never seen it before."

"Yeah, right," Audun said.

Annie reached for the vial, saying, "May I see that?" She shook it and held it up to her ear. "It's some sort of magic dust. The sound is very faint, but it's there." Turning to Liam, she took a step closer to examine his clothes. "You have some on your shirt, Liam. It almost looks as if someone blew it at you."

"There's some on the captain's clothes, too," said Millie.

Clarence began to back away, but Audun stopped him with a firm grip on his arm. "Any idea what the powder does?" he asked Annie.

"I'm not sure," she replied. "Liam, what did you say right before you went to sleep last night?"

"Good night?" he asked.

"I think this is magic dust that's meant to wipe out memories," said Annie. "It sounds very faint, so I doubt it's strong enough to last long."

"What didn't you want Liam and the captain to

81

remember?" said Annie. "That you had them change direction?"

"Why would I possibly want to do that?" Clarence asked.

"Maybe that ship has something to do with it," Millie said, pointing out to sea.

"That's a pirate flag!" said the captain. "What's a pirate ship doing all the way out here? They usually stay close to the shoreline."

"I think I can guess," said Annie. "I don't think that it's a coincidence that a pirate ship is headed our way. I bet that ship is here because Clarence told his friends that we'd be near this island on a certain day. I saw Clarence pass something to a barmaid at the tavern when we stopped to get the horseshoe replaced. I bet buying a horse wasn't the only thing he arranged. My guess is that he bought a horse just to throw us off the track. He was really sending a message to the pirates, telling them where they could find us. I think he passed something to the tavern keeper at the Rusty Nail, too."

"You *were* awfully eager to go into the Rusty Nail when Digby wanted to see us, Clarence," said Liam. "Did you pass the note when you slipped and fell? I bet you sent an update about where we'd be today. You'd know our location because you were the one telling us where to go."

"That's why you were so concerned that we were

making such good time with the wind behind us!" said Audun. "We reached the island before you said we would."

"That would explain why we're going in circles!" said Liam. "You were waiting for the pirates to show up! What were they supposed to do—hold us hostage for ransom or kill us so you could take over Dorinocco? Are these pirates friends of yours or people you hired?"

"Why should I tell you anything?" Clarence said, sneering. "You seem to think you know everything already!"

"Pardon me, Your Highness, but I can see that flag well enough to recognize it now," said the captain. "That's the *Wandering Tuna*, a pirate ship with a very bad reputation. It's getting a lot closer."

"Audun, would you mind taking my brother downstairs and locking him in his cabin?" said Liam. "Please remove all of his personal belongings and bring them up here so we can toss them overboard. Who knows what other surprises he brought with him."

"It would be my pleasure," said Audun.

"You can't throw out all my things!" Clarence whined as Audun hustled him toward the stairs. "What will I wear tomorrow?"

"Please check his pockets, too, while you're at it," Annie called to Audun. "He might have something he can use against us even now."

The captain turned the ship away from the pirates

just as a bell began to ring. Every sailor on the ship started running. "I'm calling my men to quarters," the captain told Liam. "We'll try to outrun the pirates, but their ship is faster than ours. You and your party should go below deck. If the pirates board us, we'll have to fight. My men are all brave and true, but few of them are seasoned fighters. Hide your belongings and brace yourselves. I cannot guarantee the outcome should the fight become hand to hand."

"I'm not going to hide in a cabin while you fight for us," Liam told Captain Riley. "I am going to get my sword, though. I didn't think I'd need to wear it on the ship. Annie, you and Millie should go to the cabins."

"I will if I must," Annie told him. "Just not yet."

The sails flapped as the ship turned. Sailors rushed about, trimming the lines. Within moments the sails had caught the wind again and were propelling the ship away from the pirates. The sailors who had gone below returned to the deck, bristling with cutlasses and daggers. Liam was back as well, his sword in his hand. Audun joined them a few minutes later.

"I found this hidden among Clarence's things," Audun said, handing a medallion to Liam. "Didn't I see you wearing that?"

Liam glanced at it and laughed. "Look, Annie! Clarence fell for my ruse! I didn't want him to know about the postcards," he told Audun, "so I let him think that this held the magic that took us from place to place."

"No wonder he didn't want me to throw out his things," said Audun.

Annie turned to watch the pirate ship. It had changed direction and was already pursuing them. The captain was right. The pirates did have a faster ship.

"This doesn't look good," said Millie.

In only minutes the other ship was close enough that Annie could see the pirates lining the railing, preparing to board. They looked like a nasty group with bits of bone tied in their long, filthy hair and knives stuck in their belts and in straps that crisscrossed their chests. Most carried cutlasses, although Annie saw that a few held crossbows with the bolts nocked and ready.

A big man with a bald head and a huge, bristly beard waved a cutlass in the air and shouted, "Stand down and prepare to be boarded!"

"That's Prickly Beard, one of the nastiest pirates around!" explained the captain. "The man standing beside him is Short Jack, his first mate. He's just as bad!"

"He doesn't look short to me," said Millie. "He's almost as tall as his captain."

"Oh, he's short all right," said the captain. "He just wears shoes with very thick soles. Well, I'll be jiggered. The one with red hair behind him is old Snaggle Toes.

85

A cart ran over his toes when he was just a tyke, and they've been twisted ever since. They're so bad he can't find shoes to fit, so he always goes barefoot. Last I heard he was sailing with Slippery Pete. I guess Snaggle Toes decided to change to a nastier ship. I've heard some terrible tales about what the crew of the *Wandering Tuna* does to their captives. It's enough to chill your blood and poison your dreams."

Audun gestured to Annie and Liam, drawing them aside. "I know that Millie and I promised not to reveal our dragon sides, but I think we don't have any choice now. Those pirates can destroy the *Sallie Mae* and hurt a lot of people if they get on board, but if I'm a dragon, I can cripple their ship and no one need get hurt. I'm asking you to release Millie and me from our promise."

Annie and Liam glanced at each other. "He is right, you know," said Liam. "Dragons could take care of this very quickly."

Annie sighed. "I was really hoping we could avoid this. All right," she said to Audun. "Just don't make a habit of it, please."

They hurried back to the captain, who was giving orders to some of his men.

"Captain," Audun told him. "Your men don't need to fight. Keep your ship on this course and I'll take care of the pirates."

"We will, you mean," said Millie.

The captain shook his head. "If you think you're going to talk the pirates into leaving, you're very mistaken. I've encountered men like them before and they won't give up easily."

"I don't intend to talk to them," Audun told him. "Just hold your men back so they don't get hurt."

"One man can't possibly fight them all," said the captain. "I'm not about to tell my men to stand down so you can get yourself slaughtered."

"Captain, you need to do as Audun said," said Liam. "Those pirates will be close enough to board your ship in minutes. If you listen to my friend, your ship and crew will go unharmed."

"This is absurd! No one can...Oh!" The captain's jaw dropped as Audun began to change. When a white dragon tinged with blue stood in front of him, the captain backed away until he bumped into the helm. The dragon was nearly three times longer than Captain Riley was tall, and his scales shimmered when he lowered his head to look the captain in the eyes.

"If you won't leave, at least stay out of my way," said Audun, the dragon.

"Wait for me!" Millie told her husband. A moment later, a lovely green dragon stood beside him, gently fanning her wings.

The captain turned pale, but he stood his ground when he shouted at his men, "Stand down!"

Some of the men were positioned so that they could see the dragons. As word spread, the men backed away from the railing while lowering their weapons.

Confusion reigned on the *Wandering Tuna* when the pirates who could see the dragons called out in fear. Their shipmates only saw the sailors on the *Sallie Mae* retreat, and they shouted in triumph as if they'd already won the battle. Their shouting turned to cries of panic when the dragons took to the air. A few of the braver pirates waved cutlasses above their heads when Audun swooped over the ship. With a powerful swipe of his tail, he cracked a mast, sending it toppling to the deck.

Pirates ran in every direction, but the men armed with crossbows shot one bolt after another at Audun. When Millie saw this, she tucked her wings to her sides and dove toward the ship, breathing a tongue of fire at the bolts. The bolts burst into flame and tumbled from the sky. Some fell into the ocean, hissing when they touched the water. Some landed on the deck, where sailors rushed to put out their flames. But a few fell on the sails, setting them on fire. Within moments the wind carried the flames to other parts of the ship and the fire ate its way across the decks and rigging faster than the pirates could put it out.

The pirate ship started drifting. Captain Riley hurried to steer the *Sallie Mae* away from the *Wandering Tuna*. The sailors cheered as they left the other ship behind.

Pirates jumped overboard as fire devoured their

ship. Within minutes, their captain was shouting at his men, waving his cutlass in the air. The pirates who were still on board ran to lower the longboat over the side of the *Wandering Tuna*. While the pirates climbed into the longboat, Millie and Audun returned to the deck of the *Sallie Mae*.

CHAPTER 8

THE MOMENT MILLIE TURNED back into her human form, she put her hand over her mouth and dashed down the stairs, heading back to her cabin.

"I have to go see if she's all right," said Audun, and hurried after her.

Annie and Liam stood at the stern of the ship, looking across their wake toward where they'd last seen the pirates. "I don't think they'll be coming after us now," said Annie.

Liam shook his head. "No, I don't think so, either. I'm glad they're gone, but I must say that I didn't expect Millie to set their ship on fire."

"I don't think she intended to," said Annie. "It looked as if she was just trying to protect Audun. I would have done the same thing if I was in her position and someone was aiming crossbows at you."

"That's good to know!" Liam said, pulling her close for a kiss.

"Ahem." A sailor cleared his throat. "Pardon me, Your Highness, but your brother demands to be let out of his cabin. He's making an awful racket. And the captain would like to see you as soon as it's convenient for you."

"Thank you," said Liam. "You may tell the captain that I'll be right there. You may also bring my brother up on deck. It's time he tells us if he really knows the way."

"Do you think Clarence might have been lying the whole time?" Annie asked as the sailor hurried off.

Liam shrugged. "It's possible, but it's also possible that he actually has some knowledge of the cove's location. He did spend time at sea, possibly with the very same pirates that Audun and Millie just chased off. After all that's happened, Clarence has to know that I won't stand for any more of his lies."

"Unless he thought the pirates would take care of us before we could find out that he was lying," said Annie.

"There is that," Liam said, scowling. "I swear, if I find out that he's lied about knowing how to find Skull Cove, I really might toss him overboard."

"If he's been lying, my uncle doesn't stand a chance and my father might not, either," said Annie. "We need to get medicine to them soon, and we won't be able to if we have to find someone else to show us the way."

"I'm not giving up on Clarence yet," Liam told her. "Let's hear what he has to say first."

"You have to tell me what happened!" Clarence called as soon as he came on deck. "How did you beat the pirates like that?"

It occurred to Annie that Clarence hadn't been able to see what had happened from his cabin. "He doesn't know about Millie and Audun," Annie whispered to Liam.

"Not knowing will drive him crazy!" Liam whispered back. "I don't want anyone to tell him!"

"I need to know our heading now," said the captain. "Our true heading," he added, turning to Clarence.

"First you have to tell me what happened," Clarence replied.

"No!" Liam told his brother. "You tell us the heading and I might consider answering your questions. Do you even really know where Skull Cove is located or was that just another one of your lies? If this was a trick, you're going to have a very long swim to shore."

"There you go, threatening me again!" said Clarence. "I won't tell you anything if you threaten me!"

Liam nodded as if he'd made up his mind. "Captain, please have two of your men toss my brother overboard, then we'll head to the nearest port and see if anyone there can give us directions."

"You wouldn't dare!" Clarence said as the captain gestured to two of his biggest sailors. "I'm a prince and deserve your respect!"

"You're a scoundrel and a liar and as such deserve only what I decide to give you," said Liam.

The two burly men lifted Clarence off his feet and started to carry him to the railing. "No!" Clarence shouted. "I know the way! You'll need to head west along the coastline. We'll change course again when we see the last of Viramoot."

"Very good," said the captain, and waved off his men.

Captain Riley was bringing the ship about when Clarence said to Liam, "Now you have to tell me what happened. Where did the pirates go? Why wasn't there any damage to this ship? These men all look hale and hearty. How could they fight the pirates without anyone getting hurt?"

"We won and that's all you need to know," said Liam.

"But you said you'd tell me!" Clarence cried.

"I said I'd consider it. I have and I've decided that you don't need to know the details. Gentlemen, please return my brother to his cabin," Liam told the two brawny sailors. "And make sure he stays there until I say he can come out."

႙ᴂ

Clarence was locked in his cabin for the next two days. He shouted for someone to let him out every time anyone walked past his door. Annie didn't feel sorry for him, but she did worry about Millie, who had shut herself in her cabin again. Although Annie tried to visit her friend more than once, Millie always told her that she wanted to be alone.

They didn't spot the southern tip of Viramoot until late afternoon on the third day. When Liam sent for Clarence, his brother came on deck rumpled and unshaven. "You threw out all my things!" Clarence complained. "I don't even have a comb for my hair!"

"It wouldn't have been necessary if you hadn't proven once again just how unreliable you are," Liam told him. He turned to point at the shore. "That's the last of Viramoot. Where do we go from here?"

"Head south," Clarence told the captain. "But I'll need to stay on deck if I'm to see the next landmark!" he hurried to add.

"Very well," announced Liam. "Just know that you'll be under guard every minute you're outside your cabin."

"That's fine with me," Clarence told him, "as long as I'm not stuck inside that tiny room any longer."

❧

Millie came on deck the next day, looking pale and tired. "Are you all right?" Annie asked her. "You've been seasick so long!"

"I'm fine," said Millie. "I don't think it's just seasickness. I wasn't feeling well before we came to see you, which is why we're looking for the doctor."

"I wish there was something I could do to help you," said Annie.

"Thanks," Millie replied. "But you're already doing it by helping us find Skull Cove."

"I hope the doctor is as good as your friend said he was," Annie said, thinking about her father and uncle.

"So do I," said Millie.

"Let's walk," Annie suggested. "I think the exercise will do us good. I'm curious about your kingdom. What is it like to live in Greater Greensward?"

"I love it!" said Millie. "I know there's magic in your kingdom, but not as much as in my side of the world. Most of the women in my family are witches—good ones, of course, although my grandmother and great-aunt weren't so good when the family curse took hold."

After Millie explained about the curse and how her mother had ended it, Annie plied her with questions about the kingdom. Annie was fascinated when Millie started talking about her friends. "My best friend is Zoë. She's the daughter of my mother's friend Li'l. They've known each other for ages. Li'l is a bat and her husband is a vampire prince, so Zoë can turn into a normal bat or a vampire. She doesn't drink human blood, though, and she's really nice. Zoë got engaged to my cousin Francis last month. Francis is the son of my great-aunt Grassina and her husband, Haywood. They're both witches, and so is Francis. He's also trained as a knight, and he's pretty good at magic and fighting."

"Your family and friends are so interesting! They make mine sound boring," said Annie.

"You want to hear about interesting! We have a family friend named Coral. She's a mermaid and she lives in a castle in the ocean. Her castle is near an island where a bunch of witches live."

"Unless there's more than one island like that, Liam and I have been there. It was one of the places we visited by postcard," said Annie.

"As far as I know, there's only one," said Millie. "My great-grandmother used to live on the island, but she moved back home a while ago. After she died, she moved into the dungeon with my great-grandfather. He's a ghost, too. And then there's Simon-Leo. He's a two-headed troll; each head has its own name. His mother is the troll queen and his father is a human prince, but he doesn't see his father much because his parents don't get along. And then there are the witches and fairies. They come around all the time. My mother is on the witches' council, so they hold their meetings at our castle a lot."

"I remember Azuria saying that the next meeting was going to be there," said Annie. "It sounds as if you have a very exciting life!"

"Sometimes it's too exciting!" said Millie.

Annie listened, rapt, as Millie told her about some of the things that had happened to her family. The two girls strolled about the deck, stopping now and then to look out over the waves. By late afternoon, the waves seemed to be higher and the sailing not as smooth. When Annie looked up, gray clouds were forming overhead and the wind was growing stronger.

"It looks as if a storm is headed this way," Audun told them when he came over. "You might want to go below deck."

Millie shook her head. "I've been down there too long as it is. I'm sick of that cabin. Besides, the fresh air helps me feel better."

"Promise me you'll go below if it gets much rougher," Audun said.

"I promise," said Millie. "But I won't like it."

Although Annie didn't want to go below deck any more than Millie did, the storm came on fast, and it wasn't long before the waves were so high and rough that she knew they needed to head for their cabins. They were making their way to the stairs when the waves started washing over the wooden planking. Annie clung to Millie with one arm and to a mast with the other as the storm grew fiercer. "Hold on!" Annie shouted as another wave swept toward them.

A sailor shouted, grabbing at anything he could as the water knocked him down and carried him across the deck. He caught hold of Annie's skirts and was starting to drag her down when Liam shouted, "We're coming!"

Liam's voice was faint over the crashing waves, so Annie wasn't sure that she'd heard him. "I can't hold on much longer," she shouted to Millie as another wave

followed the first and the weight of the sailor continued to pull them toward the railing.

"But I can," said Millie. Pushing away from Annie, she
let the wave carry her off, but had gone only a few yards
when she began to change. The water washing over her
shimmered. Moments later, she erupted into the air as a
dragon. With a few powerful beats of her wings, she was
at Annie's side, plucking her and the sailor out of the
water washing across the deck and carrying them to
the top of the stairs.

And then Audun the dragon was there, hauling three
half-drowned sailors. Liam came next, supporting a
sailor on either side. "This is a nasty storm!" Liam said
as a gust nearly bowled him over.

"I wish this wind would let up," Audun told him. "My
wings are tired already."

Millie gasped when the wind abruptly lessened. "Say
it again, my love," she told Audun. "Tell the wind to grow
calmer."

Audun looked puzzled when he asked, "What good
will that do?"

"Please try," Millie cried as a huge wave carried the
ship high, only to let it slide into a trough behind it.

"Anything for you," Audun said. "Grow calmer, wind."

His eyes widened and his mouth dropped open
when the wind lessened noticeably. The waves were still
rough, but it wasn't long before they decreased as well.

"Do you know what this means?" Millie asked him.

"No one else is going to get washed overboard?" said Audun.

"It's your gift! You finally learned what your special gift is!" Millie cried.

Audun grinned. "You're right! I was beginning to think that I would never have one. Well, what do you think of that?"

The water was calm enough now that the sailors were able to walk without staggering as they inspected the ship for damage and the sails for tears. One man was so relieved that the storm was over that he began to whistle a lively tune.

"What are you talking about?" Liam asked Audun. "What gift?"

"Every ice dragon has a special gift and each one is unique. Their names often reflect their gifts. My mother is named Moon Dancer and is very graceful. My father is Speedwell and he's one of the fastest fliers. Song of the Glacier is my grandmother. She can actually hear the voices of glaciers. My family all received their gifts while they were younger than I am now. I really was beginning to think it might never happen to me. Imagine—controlling the wind! Maybe I should change my name to Wind Master! Let me see what else I can do."

While his friends watched, Audun calmed the wind so there was barely a breeze.

"We need *some* wind," said Liam. "The ship won't move without it."

99

Audun nodded and muttered under his breath. A wind sprang up, moving the ship along.

"I'm so proud of you!" Millie told him. She started toward Audun, turning back into a human on the way. Suddenly she stopped, clapped her hand over her mouth, and ran to the railing. She was still feeling sick when Annie went to help her.

"I have to go lie down again," Millie groaned.

"Would you like me to come with you?" Audun asked her.

Millie shook her head. "No, I just…" Moaning, she ran to the stairs and disappeared below.

"My poor darling," said Audun. "I can't believe she's seasick again."

"I don't think she's seasick," Annie told him. "She wasn't sick at all during the storm when the water was so rough. It wasn't until she turned back into a human that she started to feel ill."

"Millie was sick so often at home that I thought she had a terrible ailment," said Audun. "Then again, she was changing between dragon and human forms all the time. It's possible that it was the change that was making her sick. I hope we find that doctor soon and that he can give us some answers."

CHAPTER 9

TWO DAYS LATER they passed a low-lying island shaped like a half circle. When Clarence saw the island, he told the captain to turn southwest. They spotted land shortly before noon the next day. Annie and Liam stayed near Clarence after that, studying the shoreline from the railing. They were sailing past a rocky promontory when the shore suddenly curved back, revealing a pretty little cove. Annie glanced at the rocks again. From this angle, they resembled the skull of a small creature. "Over there!" she cried, pointing. "That looks like a chipmunk's skull! This must be Skull Cove!"

"A chipmunk!" Clarence said with disgust. "I thought the skull would look human."

"You mean you've never been here?" asked Liam.

Clarence shook his head. "I've never been in the cove. I did sail past once. We didn't come close enough to see the skull, but a friend pointed the cove out to me."

"You surprise me, Clarence," said Liam. "I didn't know you had any friends."

"Very funny," Clarence said, looking sour. "I don't know about you, but I'm going ashore as soon as I can talk some of these sailors into taking me. Anyone else want to go?"

"We all do," said Audun. "I'll get Millie. She was feeling a little better this morning."

Annie waited impatiently while the captain brought his ship into the cove and set anchor. While they waited, Millie came on deck, looking pale and still shaky. Audun helped his wife climb into the longboat, holding her hand as the rest of their party joined them. Four sailors were going to row them to shore, then wait aboard the *Sallie Mae* until Liam summoned them back.

The water was calmer in the cove because the curve of the land protected it from the more powerful waves of the ocean. Even so, the trip to shore in the longboat seemed to take forever. The shoreline was serene with frond-topped trees on either end of a sandy beach. Annie half expected to see a cottage or hut on the beach itself, but there wasn't any sign that anyone had ever been there. When she and her party finally set foot on the shore, she wasn't sure what to do.

"Don't tell me that there is no witch doctor!" said Annie. "We can't have come all this way for nothing!"

"He probably makes his home farther inland," said

Liam. "Look at the debris on the beach. It goes all the way up to those trees. Anything built on the beach would be flooded every high tide. We need to look for a path. If the witch doctor lives near here, there's probably a path leading from the beach to his home. Let's spread out and see if we can find it."

"I think I'll sit right here," said Millie, settling onto the sand. "I don't have the strength to go slogging through the jungle right now."

"Will you be all right by yourself?" asked her husband.

Millie nodded. "The warm sand feels good. Wake me if I fall asleep."

"Clarence can go with me," said Liam.

"You don't trust me yet, brother?" asked Clarence. "I brought you here just as I promised."

"With a small detour on the way," Liam replied.

The two brothers were still arguing as they strolled down the beach together. "I guess that means I'm with you," Annie told Audun.

"Don't worry, we'll find the doctor," Audun said as they started walking in the opposite direction. "Although we'd find him a lot faster if I change. Ice dragons have a real knack for tracking. I tracked Millie from the Icy North to Greater Greensward by following her scent in the air. As long as the doctor's scent isn't too old, there shouldn't be any problem. Do you mind if I change?"

Annie glanced back at Liam and Clarence, who had

reached the edge of the trees and were studying the ground. Neither one was looking their way. "Go right ahead," she told Audun.

It took him only a moment to change. As soon as he did, he started sniffing the air.

"What do you smell now?" asked Annie.

"There's salt air, of course, and a dead fish up the beach," Audun began. "I smell seaweed, flowers, lots of vegetation, the musky scent of different kinds of animals and . . . Now, that's interesting! I smell a lot of men, not just one. We'll follow my nose and sniff out where they went."

Sand sifted into Annie's shoes as they crossed the beach. She stopped at the tree line to empty them out while Audun waited, his nose quivering. "They went this way," he said when she was ready.

Audun led the way with his head held high one moment, then nearly touching the ground the next as he sniffed the air, the trees, the undergrowth, and the ground itself. The dragon was so big that sometimes he didn't fit between the trees, so they had to backtrack and find a different way forward. Although they didn't seem to be following a path, Audun left one wherever he walked, crushing the plants, rubbing against the trees, and knocking vines to the ground with his swinging tail. Annie liked the opening he created. Without a path back to the beach, she would have been completely lost.

Something overhead called out, drawing Annie's eyes

toward the top of the trees. Furry animals with long tails and humanlike faces sat on the branches, staring down at her. When one at the back of their group shrieked, they all started swinging from branch to branch, heading deeper into the jungle.

Intent on the scent he was following, Audun didn't seem to notice the commotion. Nor did he notice the big spotted cat that appeared out of the jungle and ran away when it saw the dragon. Annie wondered if the smaller animals had been shrieking because of the cat.

"The scent is getting stronger," Audun finally said. "The men must have stopped just ahead. I smell ashes, too. Someone had a fire near here."

"Is that you, Annie?" Liam shouted from somewhere nearby.

"We're right here!" Annie called back.

"I'd better change," Audun whispered to her. "Clarence still doesn't know that Millie and I are dragons."

"Your secret might be impossible to keep for very long," Annie said while he turned back into a human.

"I know, but I'm going to try," replied Audun as he straightened the clothes on his human body.

They didn't have much farther to go before they stepped out of the jungle into a clearing and saw Liam and Clarence. Millie was there as well, peering into one of the four grass huts that stood in a circle around a central fire. "There you are!" she said when she saw them. "Liam and Clarence found a short path that led straight here. They came across an enormous snake as big around as a man, so they got worried and went back to get me. What took you so long? We've been here awhile."

"We got sidetracked," said Annie, not wanting to mention that they'd been following a dragon's nose. "Is the doctor here? Have you seen him?"

Liam shook his head. "We've looked in all the huts, but no one is here and the ashes in the fire pit are cold. The smaller huts are set up for sleeping. They're probably for his patients. It looks as if the big hut is the one Ting-Tang uses. That's where we found something interesting."

Annie and Audun followed Liam to the biggest hut and looked inside. The space was cluttered with vials, bottles, and jars covering three low tables. Larger jars were stacked against the walls and a big pot of something gray bubbled on a table of its own. When Annie spotted broken vials on the floor and a jar lying on its side, leaking yellow goo, she knew that something was wrong. "What do you suppose happened here?" she asked.

"It looks as if there was a scuffle," said Liam.

"Someone fought with the doctor and took him away," Audun suggested. "See those marks on the doorframe? I think someone was holding on to the door while someone else tried to drag him outside. Maybe those men I smelled on the way here kidnapped the doctor."

"You smelled some men?" asked Liam.

Annie glanced outside to make sure that Clarence

couldn't hear them. "We followed their scent here. Audun has a very good sense of smell when he's a dragon."

"I see," said Liam. "Then maybe you'd like to track whoever took the doctor and see if you can find him. We need to start for home as soon as possible."

"I can do that," Audun replied. "Please tell Millie that I'll be right back. I'll see what I can find from the air. I shouldn't be gone long."

"I'll go talk to Millie," said Liam, and left the hut with Audun.

Alone in the grass hut, Annie decided that she might as well look around. Generally, she didn't like to snoop in other people's homes, but this felt different somehow. It wasn't so much a home as a work space, with the ingredients of the doctor's trade evident in the jars and bottles and the strange things hanging from the posts that supported the roof. Long thin strips dangled from the ceiling on one side of the hut. When Annie took a closer look, she discovered that they were snake skins of varying lengths and colors. Dried herbs and grasses hung in another part of the hut alongside dried flowers that gave off the most intoxicating scent. Annie found jars filled with dried insects, including beetles as big as her fist and iridescent blue butterflies that were almost as big. Crushed red leaves filled another jar, and sticky golden sap glistened in a clay pot.

When Annie came across a folded sleeping mat made of woven grasses, she decided that it might be someone's home after all. She was leaving the hut when she heard Liam shout and followed his voice to one of the smaller grass structures. When she stepped inside, Liam was wrestling his brother to the floor.

"What happened?" she asked, stepping out of the way as Clarence flailed about, nearly kicking her.

"I left him alone for a few minutes and he got into trouble," Liam said as he wrapped a piece of rope around Clarence's wrists, tying them together. "I found him rifling one of the huts, stealing Ting-Tang's belongings."

"The place is abandoned!" said Clarence. "Anyone could come along and take these things. Why shouldn't it be someone who could actually use them?"

"What did you take?" Annie asked as she watched Liam tie his brother's ankles.

"I don't know—some weird stuff wrapped in leaves and a wooden mask."

"First of all," said Liam, "these buildings weren't abandoned. The man was probably kidnapped. And second, these things still belong to him. It amazes me how you remind everyone that you're a prince when you think it will help you, but act like a common thief when the mood strikes."

"It was only a few souvenirs!" said Clarence.

"You don't take souvenirs from someone's home!" Annie told him.

"Where is everyone?" shouted a voice.

"Audun's back!" Annie cried.

"Where did he go?" asked Clarence.

"To look for the doctor, of course!" Annie told him.

"Clarence can stay here. Annie, come with me," Liam said, taking her by the hand.

Clarence grunted and tried to roll over, but it wasn't easy with his hands and feet bound. "You're not going to leave me like this, are you? What if I need a drink of water? Or what if that giant snake comes back?"

"I tied you up to keep you out of trouble. We can't very well ask the doctor for help if you're stealing from him! Don't worry, we won't be gone long," Liam told him from the doorway. "I'll shut the door. That should keep the snakes out."

CHAPTER 10

AUDUN WAS A HUMAN again and was standing in the center of the circle near the fire pit. He was frowning when Annie and Liam joined him.

"I found the doctor, or at least I think I did," said Audun. "He's in a pit at the edge of a village deep in the jungle. I couldn't get close enough to see into the pit because a group of men armed with spears surrounded it. Every time I tried to get close, they threw their spears at me. I was afraid that a spear might fall into the pit and hurt the doctor, so I came back to get you."

"And you think Liam and I can get him out?" said Annie.

Audun nodded. "It should be easy. I'll draw the men away and you two can rescue the witch doctor."

"How deep is this pit?" asked Liam.

"I'm not sure," said Audun. "I couldn't get a good look.

I saw plenty of strong vines while I was looking for the doctor. Tie a couple of those together and you've got a sturdy rope."

"What about Clarence and Millie?" Annie asked.

"Clarence can stay tied up in the hut. Last I saw, Millie was asleep in a hut by herself," said Liam.

"She's exhausted," said Audun. "I don't think she got a single good night's sleep during the entire voyage. I'd like to let her keep sleeping if we can. If I could find something to write on, I'd leave her a note. Have you seen anything I could use?"

Annie shook her head. "No, I haven't."

Audun scratched the dirt with his shoe. "I suppose I could write on the dirt outside the hut. Give me a minute and I'll be ready to go."

Annie and Liam waited while Audun found a stick and wrote a note to Millie. When he was finished, he checked on his wife one last time before returning to his friends. "Where exactly is this village?" asked Annie.

"I can take you there," said Audun, "but we should leave the clearing if you don't want Clarence to see or hear us."

"Why should we...Oh, I see!" Annie said. Millie had given Annie and Liam a ride as a dragon once. It had been one of the most exciting and exhilarating things Annie had ever done. If Audun was offering to give them a ride, Annie wasn't about to turn him down.

Annie and Liam followed Audun into the jungle. They were scarcely out of sight of the huts when Audun said, "This is far enough."

He took a few steps away from them to a spot where the trees were farther apart. Annie held her breath as the air shimmered, and then Audun the dragon was there. "I didn't realize you were so much bigger than Millie," Liam said as he helped Annie climb onto the ice dragon's back.

"I've been going through a growth spurt," Audun told them. "Dragons grow our entire lives. Even my grand-parents are still growing. You should see the king of the fire-breathing dragons. He's ancient and the biggest dragon I've ever met. Are you settled back there?"

After Liam wrapped his arms around her from behind, Annie said that she was ready. She could feel the ice dragon bunch his muscles under her. Then sud-denly he was launching himself into the air, spreading his wings with a snap. Annie and Liam bent low as Audun carried them between the trees. And then they were above the jungle canopy and could look down on the trees spread out below. It made Annie think of a vast green blanket edged with the ocean on one side and mountains in the far-off distance. Here and there rivers meandered across the jungle, relieving the green with a touch of blue. A flock of red and yellow birds flew just above the trees, their long tails trailing behind them. They didn't seem to notice Audun until his shadow passed over them, making them squawk and disappear back into the foliage.

When he reached a broad river of a particularly clear blue, Audun turned to follow it. Tracing the river from above, they continued on until they reached the narrower line of a small tributary. This water was muddy colored, but it was still distinctive among the trees. As they moved farther up the smaller river, the ground below them began to rise. Angling higher, they skimmed above a narrow waterfall and saw that the surrounding land was becoming rocky and uneven. A long section of rapids churned the water to froth, calming when they rounded another bend.

Audun finally left the river behind, heading toward a gap in the jungle. He started circling then, going lower with each pass. Turning his head toward his friends, Audun shouted, "We'll land here and I'll tell you what we'll do next. I don't want to go too close, so we'll have to walk a bit. Hold on!"

Liam tightened his hold around Annie, and they both bent low over the dragon's neck as Audun angled more steeply toward the ground. And then the trees were rushing past and Audun slowed his descent with a few beats of his wings.

Annie couldn't stop smiling as Liam helped her off the dragon's back. "That was so much fun!" she said.

"And fast," said Liam. "It would have taken us days to travel that far by foot."

"Thank you!" Annie said as the dragon lowered his head to their level.

Audun shrugged. "You're helping Millie and me as much as we're helping you. There's a village over there," he said, pointing. "And the pit is that way." He pointed in a different direction. "After we make a rope out of these vines, I'll go to the village to distract the people while you take the rope and climb down into the pit to bring up the witch doctor."

"You never did say why you think he's in the pit," said Liam. "And wouldn't it be easier if you just went down there and got him?"

"I know he's down there because there's magic covering the pit," said Audun. "And I can't go down there because, well, I just can't."

"I thought dragon magic was stronger than any other kind," said Annie.

"It is," said Audun. "But I'll frighten him if I go down there as a dragon. I'll have to become human. I've never told you this before, but when I'm in my frail human body, I'm afraid of a lot of things that don't bother me when I'm a dragon, including heights." He looked away then, as if too embarrassed to meet their eyes.

"But you fly so high when you're a dragon!" Annie cried.

"I know, but as a human I can't go very high without getting all sweaty and making my heart race."

"I had no idea," said Annie.

"Only Millie knows," Audun told her. "Please don't mention it to anyone else."

Annie glanced at Liam, then back at Audun. "We wouldn't dream of it!" she told him.

"Vines, huh?" Liam said, gazing up into the trees. "Any chance you could help us collect them before you go distract the villagers?"

"It would be my pleasure," said Audun.

While the dragon snapped vines with his talons, Annie and Liam collected the pieces, making a big pile. Liam showed Annie how to tie a strong knot that wouldn't come apart, so it didn't take long to make an extra-long rope. They added knots in the rope every few feet to help the climbers. After coiling up the rope, Liam carried most of it over his shoulder. Annie followed behind, lugging the rest in her arms. When they started in the direction of the pit, Audun headed for the village. Annie knew when he got there, because that was when the screaming started. They hid while people who had been near the pit ran past them toward the village to see what was going on.

"We should hurry," said Liam when the area around the pit was quiet. "There's no telling how long he'll be able to distract the villagers."

"I'm following you," Annie told him. The mosquitoes had found them, and their constant biting was starting to make her irritable. When she swatted one on her arm, she nearly dropped the vines.

115

The pit wasn't very far from where Audun had landed. Liam nearly fell in when the path ended abruptly at the opening. "Watch out!" he cried, staggering backward. "The ground is crumbling around the edges. Why would anyone dig a big pit on a path like this?"

"Either they wanted to trap people," said Annie, "or no one dug it. The edges are crumbling like you said. I think this is a naturally occurring sinkhole. No one put this thing here."

"What's a sinkhole?" asked Liam.

"A place where the ground drops away, leaving a big hole. Usually there's a cave or empty space underneath."

Liam stepped closer to peer into the hole. "Hello! Is anyone there?" he shouted.

No one answered.

Annie moved to stand beside Liam. The pit was at least forty feet across and pitch-black inside. Even the top of the hole's walls were so black that she couldn't see anything.

"I guess we'll have to go down and look around," said Annie. "I hate climbing with ropes!"

"I don't blame you after what happened with the witch and the crows at that tower," Liam said. "You stay here and I'll go down the rope. If the witch doctor is there like Audun said, I should be back up soon."

"If you don't mind . . . ," said Annie.

Liam bent down to give her a quick kiss. "You know

I like climbing. Let me tie one end to a tree, and I'll head down."

Liam soon had the vine secured around a sturdy trunk. Annie kept out of his way when he walked to the edge of the sinkhole and tossed the rest of the rope over the side. She gasped when it bounced and flew back at Liam.

"Ow!" he said, rubbing his chest where it had hit him.

Annie stepped closer to the pit and leaned down to listen. "I'm sorry, that's my fault," she told Liam after a moment. "I should have been paying attention. I forgot that Audun said there was magic over the pit. I can hear it now. It's odd, though; almost as if there are two tunes playing."

"And it's there to keep people out?" asked Liam.

"I guess," said Annie. Sighing, she reached for the end of the rope. "I really hate this."

The vines were heavy, but after a few tries Annie was able to push the rope over the edge. Because she was still touching part of the rope, the magic didn't do anything, and it fell down into the pit, tugging the end that was tied to the tree.

"Wish me luck!" she said, trying not to show how frightened she felt.

"Just a minute," said Liam. "You got the rope in the hole. Maybe if you hold on to this end, the magic won't stop me and I can go down there now."

Liam turned around to hold on to the rope and tried

to step over the edge. Unfortunately, his foot couldn't seem to go past the top of the hole. "It's almost as if it has a lid on it," Liam said, tapping his foot against what looked like open air.

"Then it really is up to me," said Annie.

Liam looked worried. "I wish I was going instead of you."

Annie laughed. She grabbed hold of the rope and started down. "So do I!" she told him.

As Annie descended, her feet were swallowed in darkness. Seeing her legs disappear was disconcerting, so she closed her eyes as she lowered herself down the rope. She could hear the melody of the magic, but it grew fainter even as an incessant pounding grew louder the lower she went. The dark behind her eyelids seemed to lessen as she descended, then disappeared entirely when she was only a few yards down. The pounding was louder now, making her heart beat with the rhythm.

Opening her eyes, she found that she was just below a layer of gray that turned black again now that she had left it. Within moments it was as dark as it had been before she entered it and looked like a ceiling painted black. The area she was in now was as bright as day, almost as if she was aboveground and not in a hole at all. She could look down all the way to the bottom, which didn't seem quite as far as she'd feared.

Apparently, the pit that had looked circular from above was much more uneven inside. The wall she was descending was made of rock with bulges and crevices all the way down. At the base, the center of the pit was filled with water. Aside from some shade-loving plants and a few lost birds, there was very little down there except a long-tailed animal like those she'd seen in the trees, and a man pounding on wooden bowls covered with animal hides. The animal was dancing around the man, whose head was thrown back with his eyes closed. Annie doubted that either of them had noticed she was there.

The rope swayed as Annie lowered herself another few feet. Closing her eyes again helped, so she went down most of the way without seeing where she was going. Suddenly the drumming stopped. Annie opened her eyes and saw that the man and the animal were looking up at her.

"Who are you?" he called. "What do you want?"

"My name is Annie," she said, dropping the rest of the way until she was standing on her feet. "I'm here to rescue you."

"Why?" he asked. "I don't know you." The little animal jumped into the man's arms and climbed onto his shoulder.

"You are the witch doctor Ting-Tang, aren't you?" she asked. The man nodded and stood up. He was shorter than Annie; the top of his head reached her shoulders. His dark hair was almost as long as Annie's and he had it pulled back into a ponytail. A necklace of seashells covered much of his otherwise bare chest and he wore a loincloth made of skin that looked as if it might have belonged to a spotted cat like the one she'd seen. His bright blue eyes were in sharp contrast to skin tanned a dark, warm brown. When he grinned, his teeth flashed white.

"I am Ting-Tang," he said. "But my parents named me Arnold when I was born. You have the accent of someone from Treecrest. Is that where you're from?"

"It is," said Annie. Ting-Tang clapped his hands in delight. "I knew it! It's been so long since I've talked to someone from my old home. Where do you live in Treecrest?"

"The castle, actually," said Annie. "I'm Princess Annabelle. We need you to help my father, King Halbert, and my uncle, Prince Rupert. They are both very ill and none of the doctors or herbalists in the kingdom can help them. Some friends of mine told me about you. They're here also, seeking your help for a problem of their own."

"I'd love to help you, but I'm in a bit of a bind," Ting-Tang said. "The villagers who brought me here won't let me go. They said it's such a long trip that they want to keep me here in case someone else gets sick."

"Are there many sick people here? It isn't the plague, is it?"

"Nothing like that," said Ting-Tang. "If it were the plague, I'd have cured it long ago. No, it's little things like toothaches, bunions, and boils. Simple stuff that drove me from my home in Treecrest in the first place."

"How could things like that drive you away?" asked Annie.

"I grew tired of treating them, but that's all people wanted me for. I was twelve years old when I came into my magic. I was so young that people didn't trust me to take care of anything more serious than their minor ailments. After a while, I wanted to test my skills, so I ran away from home and signed on as the doctor aboard a sailing ship. Cut it out, Chee Chee!" he told the little animal as it climbed atop his head.

"What kind of animal is that?" asked Annie. "I saw more like him in the jungle near your home."

"He's a monkey," said Ting-Tang. "He fell out of a tree when he was just a baby. I set his broken leg and raised him after that. He goes wherever I go now. As I was saying, I signed on as doctor on a sailing ship. One day there was a terrible storm and we were shipwrecked just off the coast of Skull Cove. When another ship found us, the others left, but I liked it here, so I stayed behind. I've been practicing my magic here ever since. Someday I'll get it right." He grinned and slapped his thighs. "That was a little witch doctor humor. I'm a little witch doctor, so …"

"I get it," said Annie. "Are you as good as people say? My friend told me that a witch named Mudine thinks you're wonderful."

"I'm not only good, I'm the best! What's wrong with your father and the prince?"

"We call it the creeping blue. It started out with their feet turning blue. They lost their appetites, too, then the blue slowly crept up their bodies. When it got higher, the pain set in. My grandfather died from the disease when my father and his brother were young."

"Hmm," Ting-Tang said, tapping his chin. "That's very serious. Fortunately for you, I've actually treated the disease before. Successfully, I might add. So, how do you propose to rescue me?"

"We'll climb up this rope," Annie said, giving it a tug. "My husband is waiting up there and so is our friend Audun." She stopped talking and turned around in surprise when the monkey started pounding on the drums while looking expectantly at Ting-Tang.

"Not now, Chee Chee," said the witch doctor. "I'll dance while you play later. I'm trying to have a conversation with this nice lady now."

The monkey's cheerful face fell when he stopped playing. Turning his back on Annie and Ting-Tang, he sat with his head down and his shoulders hunched.

"Tell me," Ting-Tang said to Annie, "if your husband is up there, why didn't he come down here instead of you?"

"Because magic can't touch me," said Annie. "I'm the only one who could get past your magic spell."

"Oh, that! I guess I made it too strong. It wasn't supposed to keep people out, just snakes. They were always falling over the edge into the pit. I hate snakes! Lizards, too, for that matter. Any reptile, really, although I don't mind turtles."

"Why are you down here?" Annie asked.

"Because of my drums," said Ting-Tang. "They help me relax, but the tribe members say the music I make is annoying. You see, the day they came to kidnap me, they tied me hand and foot to a long pole. I'd had too much coconut milk the night before, so my magic wasn't working very well. They were about to cart me off like a wild boar when I told them I would help them only if they let me bring my drums. When I convinced them that they needed my cooperation, they agreed and brought them along. Unfortunately, after listening to me play, they tossed my drums into the pit. I came down here after them, and found that the sound was better here than up above. When they still complained, I blocked the sound from leaving the pit. If I let you rescue me, my drums will have to come, too."

"I think that can be arranged," said Annie. "But how are you going to get them out of the pit?"

"Leave that to me," Ting-Tang replied.

"Will it involve magic?" asked Annie. "Because if it does, I should probably go up first so your magic will work."

"No magic, but I will use the extra vine you have lying there." Ting-Tang's fingers flew as he undid the last length of vine from the rope that was lying on the ground. Wrapping the middle around his waist, he tied the ends to his two drums. "I'll go first. See you on top!"

Ting-Tang held out his hand and said in a soft voice, "Chee Chee!" The little monkey turned to look at him. Seeing the outstretched hand, he perked up and ran to Ting-Tang, who set him on his shoulder. As agile as a squirrel, the little witch doctor scurried up the vine rope with his drums dangling from his waist and the monkey clinging to his neck.

Annie stood below, watching him. As soon as Ting-Tang reached the black ceiling, it fizzled and disappeared. The melody of the magic was gone, as was the light that had brightened the bottom of the pit. Sunlight reached only one side now, leaving the rest in deep shadow.

Once Ting-Tang had clambered over the edge of the pit, Annie started up. She cringed when a snake slithered over the edge and fell past her, twisting and turning in the empty air.

"Ting-Tang was right," she murmured when she heard another one land behind her. "Snakes do fall in here a lot. If he's so afraid of snakes and lizards, I wonder what he'll think about getting a ride from a dragon."

CHAPTER 11

HAND OVER HAND, Annie climbed up the rope using the wall of the pit for toeholds when she could. She looked up now and then to see how much farther she had left to go, and was nearing the top when she saw Liam silhouetted in the bright daylight behind him. Annie was only feet from the edge when he reached down and pulled her up the rest of the way.

She blinked and her eyes adjusted as she looked around. Liam was beside her and Audun was there as a human again, standing next to Ting-Tang. Annie was about to ask why they were just standing there when she realized that they weren't alone. At least twenty spear-carrying men surrounded them.

The fiercest-looking man pointed at Annie and said, "What fools would bring a girl on a raiding party?"

Annie wasn't sure, but it looked to her as if the

movements of the man's mouth didn't match up with the words coming out of it.

"They aren't here to steal from you," said Ting-Tang. "They came to rescue me."

"They came to steal you, you mean," said the man. "You're our witch doctor now."

Annie decided that he must be the headman if he was doing all the talking.

Ting-Tang shook his head. "I've told you before, I'm not staying here forever. I'm happy I was able to help your tribe, but I need to get back to my hut. I have other patients coming to see me. These people came looking for me because they need medical assistance."

"They look fine to me," said the headman, although his mouth looked as if it was saying something much longer and more involved.

"We came to get help for my father and my uncle," Annie told the man. "They are both very sick and will die without Ting-Tang's help."

"Why should that matter to us?" said the man. "We do not know these people. If it is your father, he is already old. He has probably lived longer than most of our people do."

"My wife needs help as well," Audun told them. "She is expecting our first child and is very ill."

"A baby!" said the man. "That is different!"

"The people of the tribe treasure children because

they have so few," Ting-Tang whispered to Annie while the tribesmen talked among themselves.

"What's with their mouths?" Annie whispered back. "Why don't they match up with their words?"

"I cast a spell so I could understand them and they could understand me," said Ting-Tang. "I think it works rather well, don't you?"

"We have decided that you may leave on one condition," said the headman. "After the baby is born, you must give it to us."

"I'm not giving my baby to anyone!" Audun declared.

"Then you may never leave," the headman told him.

"This is ridiculous," said Audun. "I felt bad about scaring your women and children back at your village. I hoped you might be reasonable about letting us go now, but apparently I was wrong. We're taking Ting-Tang back with us and you can't stop us or keep us here."

The headman opened his mouth to say something, but the air around Audun was already shimmering. When he turned into a full-size dragon, some of the men shouted and ran away, but the rest raised their spears, ready to fight.

"Hold your breath!" he shouted to his friends.

Ting-Tang looked confused and didn't respond right away, but Annie and Liam took deep breaths and held them as Audun puffed poison gas at the tribesmen.

A moment later, the tribesmen were all gagging. Ting-Tang was, too, and his little monkey had collapsed on the ground.

Audun thought for a second and said, "Light breeze, please!"

A breeze strong enough to ruffle the leaves sprang up, carrying away the remnants of the gas. When it was gone, Annie and Liam started breathing again, but the others were suffering from the effects of the poison. It hadn't been enough to kill them, but it had made them all very nauseous.

"Climb on my back," Audun told Annie and Liam.

"What about him?" Annie asked, gesturing to Ting-Tang, who was still vomiting.

"I don't want him on my back if he's doing that," said Audun, "so I guess I'll carry him with my talons."

"As sick as he is, I don't think he'll care either way," Liam declared.

"Don't forget his monkey!" called Annie.

As soon as Annie and Liam were settled on Audun's back, he picked up Chee Chee with the talons on his left front foot and Ting-Tang with the talons on his right. The drums still hung from the witch doctor's waist, and they banged together as the dragon took off. None of the tribesmen looked up as Audun rose above the trees and turned toward the coast.

"I followed the rivers here before, but this time I'm going straight back," Audun said over his shoulder.

128

"You can do that?" Liam shouted.

"Once a dragon has gone somewhere, he can find the location again," said Audun. "The more a dragon visits it, the stronger the connection. I should find Ting-Tang's huts pretty easily this time."

They were flying over the jungle with the ocean in the distance when Ting-Tang started thrashing around. "Stop that," Audun shouted, giving him a shake. "I'm taking you home. We'll be there in a few minutes."

"You mean you aren't taking me back to your cave to eat me?" Ting-Tang shouted back.

"Oh, gross!" said Audun. "I've never eaten a human in my life. I don't know anyone who has, either. Humans smell funny and I'm sure they taste worse. Ice dragons eat fish and some meat, not people! Stop wiggling or I might drop you!"

Ting-Tang stopped moving, although he did turn his head to look at Audun. "You've really never eaten anyone?"

"Never!" said Audun. "My wife would never forgive me if I did."

꒰ꞈ

Millie was standing outside the huts, waiting for them when they landed. She looked relieved to see them, and went running up to Audun before he'd even closed his wings. "I was so worried," she cried. "You left without telling me you were going!"

"You were asleep and I thought you needed your rest. I scratched a note for you in the dirt. See—right there! Oh, I guess you walked all over it. You can't read it now. I'm sorry you were worried, but we were gone only a few hours."

"You were gone half a day! I was here all by myself and I didn't know what was going on."

"You weren't by yourself," said Audun. "Clarence was here. He was tied up in a hut."

"There's no one here but me," Millie told him.

"Didn't you look in the other huts?" asked Liam. "Clarence was right here." Liam went into the hut where he'd left Clarence tied up. He came back out a few seconds later. "He's gone. I found the rope, but Clarence and that wooden mask are missing."

"He can't have gone far," said Audun. "I'll see if I can find him."

"Don't go yet," Millie told him. "Let's hear what the doctor has to say first."

Ting-Tang had already taken Chee Chee into the bigger hut. When Annie peeked inside, the witch doctor was cradling the little monkey in his arms. Chee Chee was clinging to him, whimpering and shivering. Looking up, Ting-Tang saw Annie. "Your dragon friend really frightened him."

"I'm sorry," said Annie, "but we had to leave in a hurry. I'm sure Audun wouldn't have used his poison gas if he could have thought of any other way. Would you be able to talk to us now? We have to leave for home as soon as we can."

The witch doctor nodded as he set the monkey in a basket made up as a little bed. "I'm grateful that you helped me return home. I would have gotten away from the tribe eventually, but they weren't going to let me go without a fight, and that's something I try to avoid. If an upset stomach is the worst thing that happened, I think we all got off lightly."

"What will you do if the tribe comes back for you?" Annie asked as he started for the door.

"Don't worry about me. Now that I know it's a possibility, there are precautions that I can take."

Millie and Audun were standing together, talking in soft voices, when he walked out. They turned to look at him, and reached for each other's hands. "Let's start with you, young lady," he told Millie. "I assume you're married to our dragon-man. Do you turn into a dragon as well?"

"I do," she said, nodding.

"Congratulations on your impending motherhood," said Ting-Tang. "Your husband told me that you've been getting ill. Is it usually after you've changed from one form to another?"

"It is. It lasts a few days, then I'm fine again," Millie told him.

"Then it's very simple," said Ting-Tang. "Don't change. Choose one form and keep it until the baby is born. It will be better for you and your baby. Get plenty of rest and don't exert yourself. I have a potion I can give you in case you get queasy now and then."

"That sounds easy," said Audun, putting his arms around Millie.

"I'm going to stay human," Millie told him. "I've been around enough pregnant women to know what to expect. I have no idea what dragons go through."

"And now for you," Ting-Tang said as he turned to Annie. "Curing the Blue Death is easy, too. All you need is very pure water and a giant pearl. You must steep the pearl in the water as it boils for one hour, then the patients must drink the liquid. You're very lucky. There's a giant pearl close by. A powerful witch stole it from a sea monster years ago. A sea witch brought it here. Years later, her mother followed her and they fought. Their magic got all jumbled up, and they've made the same ten minutes repeat over and over again. Unfortunately, now anyone who goes too close is trapped in those ten minutes as well."

"I've heard the story about the theft of the pearl many times," said Millie. "If it's the same pearl, my mother was the witch who took it. Do you know if the two sea witches were named Pearl and Nastia Nautica?"

"Yes, indeed," said Ting-Tang.

"If the sea witches are trapped in a magic spell, I'll be

the one to go fetch the pearl," said Annie. "Anyone else would get caught in the time loop with them."

"You're not going alone," Liam told her. "I won't let you."

"We'll see," Annie replied. "But before we decide who else is going, we have to find out exactly what we're getting into."

CHAPTER 12

"THAT ELIXIR TASTED awful, but I feel so much better now!" Millie announced to Audun and her friends.

"I don't think you should go with us," said Audun. "You've met Nastia Nautica and know how truly horrible she can be."

"I do know," said Millie, "and I still think I should go. I've never met her daughter, Pearl, but my mother knows her. She might be more willing to listen to me than to complete strangers."

"Are you sure you shouldn't stay here and rest?" Audun asked her.

Millie shook her head. "I had cabin fever from staying in the cabin on the ship for so long. Now I think I've developed hut fever. If I rest any more I'm going to go crazy. I need to go somewhere and do something!"

"She can go to the beach with us, then decide if she wants to go farther," said Ting-Tang.

At the mention of the beach, Chee Chee came racing out of the hut and leaped into Ting-Tang's arms. "All right," the witch doctor said, laughing. "You can go, too, but we'll take your carry sack with us this time."

They all waited while Ting-Tang went into his hut, returning a moment later with a sack made of woven seagrass. Dropping to one knee, he held the bag open while Chee Chee climbed inside. With the sack draped over his neck and shoulder, the witch doctor led the way into the jungle. Instead of following one of the paths that his visitors had used, he took another path that cut through the jungle for what seemed like miles. When they finally emerged from among the trees, they were on the edge of a larger bay where the water ran deeper and wasn't as protected from the ocean waves.

"Skull Cove is just past that promontory," Ting-Tang said, pointing. "The path we took is easier than walking along the beach. You can't see it from here, of course, but if you were to go straight ahead from this spot, you'd find a shipwreck about thirty feet down. It's the ship I was on when that storm hit. Everyone got off all right, but the ship sank within minutes. The sea witch Pearl made her home in it. That's where she and her mother are arguing even now. If you wait here long enough, you'll—"

BOOM! Something exploded underwater, sending a geyser into the air. "That was it!" said Ting-Tang. "They keep having the same fight over and over. Stay here another ten minutes and you'll see it again."

135

"Are you saying that we have to go underwater to get the pearl?" asked Annie.

"That's where it is," Ting-Tang told her. "Inside the shipwreck with Pearl."

"How do you know that it's there? Or that they keep having the same argument?" asked Liam.

"Because I went down there to investigate," said Ting-Tang. "I was looking for something I'd left in the ship, but found the two sea witches instead. I stayed long enough to see what they were doing and haven't been back since."

"Why didn't you get stuck in the time loop with them?" asked Liam.

"I kept my distance," said Ting-Tang, "but the fish that swam past me got stuck. Anyone who goes close enough to get the pearl would get stuck, too."

"I can swim," said Annie, "but I don't think I can hold my breath long enough to look around."

"You won't have to," declared Audun. "One of the ice dragon king's advisors gave me this amulet so I could do a job for them." Reaching into the neck of his tunic, he pulled up a chain holding an embossed amulet and showed it to his friends. Crashing waves surrounded a round bubble on the front of the amulet; it looked so lifelike that Annie could swear the waves were moving. "I'll wear this when we go underwater. It will allow me to breathe as if I were still on dry land. Whoever is touching me will be able to as well."

"And the amulet will work around me because it's dragon magic?" said Annie.

Audun nodded. "And I'll go as a dragon, so we'll get there much faster. Dragons are powerful swimmers."

"I'm going, too," said Millie. "I'll explain to Pearl why we need to borrow the giant pearl. I'm sure she'll let us take it if I mention Mother. Don't you think that's funny? We're getting a pearl from Pearl!"

"I'm afraid I'll think it's funnier after my father and Uncle Rupert drink the potion," said Annie. "I just want to get home to give it to them."

"I'm sorry," Millie said, giving her a sympathetic look. "I didn't mean to make light of it, but I feel so relieved that Ting-Tang told me what to do that I forgot we still have to get medicine for your family."

"I guess we're all going," said Liam.

"Not me," said Ting-Tang. "You don't need me there and I'm not a very good swimmer. It took me a while to work up the courage the last time I went."

"You're not going, either, Liam," said Audun. "The amulet can work for three people at once, but I think four might be too many. I don't want to get down there only to find out someone isn't getting enough air."

"But who's going to watch out for Annie?" he asked.

"We will!" said Millie. "Two dragons can handle anything."

"You can't change, remember?" Audun told her.

Millie's hand flew to her mouth. "I forgot already!

137

This pregnancy thing is going to be harder than I thought!"

"I'll be fine," said Annie. "The sea witches' magic won't work on me. I'll be back before you know it, Liam."

BOOM! The geyser shot out of the water again.

"We just wasted ten minutes," said Audun. He glanced at the sky and frowned. "We need to hurry if we're going to do this before dark." Stepping away from his friends, Audun gave his wife a smile, then turned to face the bay as he changed into a dragon again.

The air was still shimmering around the ice dragon when Ting-Tang shook his head in amazement. "Fascinating! I'll never get tired of seeing that. Stop scratching me, Chee Chee! The dragon isn't going to hurt you!"

Frightened, the monkey had climbed out of the bag and was clinging to Ting-Tang, pressing his little face against the man's shoulder. Patting the monkey, Ting-Tang turned back to Annie. "You should be fine as long as you get in and out as quickly as you can. Go down into the hold and head toward the stern. That's the back of the ship. You'll see an open door straight ahead. The sea witches will be too busy fighting, so they won't see you if you're careful. Grab the pearl—you'll know when—and get out of there. Don't hang around, because the pearl's absence will change things and you don't want to be there when that happens. Here, take this with you so you can carry the pearl while you swim," he said, handing the seagrass sack to Annie. "Good luck! Chee Chee and I will be here when you come back up. Oh, while you're there, if you happen to see a blue bowl, I'd appreciate it if you brought it back, too. I could really use that now."

"You two ladies should climb onto my back," said Audun. "It's the best way to keep us together."

Millie was already making herself comfortable on her husband's back when Liam gave Annie a boost up. She settled down behind Millie, trying not to sit on the sharper scales.

"Hold on to me!" Millie said over her shoulder as Audun started toward the water.

Annie wrapped her arms around Millie's waist and held on tight. Although her friends were convinced that the magic of the amulet would help them breathe, she held her breath as the ice dragon plunged into the waves. Peering through the murky water, she tried to see the sunken ship, but all she spotted were fish that darted away when they got a good look at Audun.

Annie was still holding her breath when Millie turned her head and said, "Breathe! I know you're holding your breath, but the amulet really does work."

Annie nodded. *It must work if Millie can talk underwater,* she told herself. Even though her mind said it was all right, her body didn't want to let go of her last gasp of air. She had to force herself to exhale and take in the smallest breath. To her surprise, it felt like she was outside on a rainy day. The air was humid, but not too bad. Relieved, she took a deeper breath, then laughed out loud and gave Millie a squeeze.

"It does work!" she exclaimed. "This is wonderful!"

"Is that the ship?" Millie asked, pointing straight ahead.

Annie looked over her friend's shoulder. "I think so," she said, wishing the water were clearer.

Audun was already heading toward the dark shape on the bottom of the bay. Annie was trying to see which end of the ship was the back when Millie started to squirm.

"What's wrong?" Audun asked, whipping his head around.

"I don't feel well again," said Millie. "I'm sorry. I thought I could do this, but I don't think I can."

Audun glanced from Millie to Annie, appearing unsure of what to do.

"Give me the amulet and take her back to shore," said Annie. "Ting-Tang made it sound very straightforward. I can do this myself."

"I don't think—" Audun began.

"I'll be fine," Annie said as she started to get off his back. "I need that amulet, though."

Audun nodded his great scaly head. "I'll be right back. Hold your breath, Millie. I'll have you in fresh air in no time!"

Using his talons, Audun yanked off the amulet and

140

handed it to Annie even as he started to head back to the surface. Wondering if she'd done the right thing, Annie pulled the chain over her head and tucked the amulet into the neckline of her gown.

Turning to face the bottom of the bay, Annie started swimming. She had learned how to swim from the stable boys at her parents' castle and had spent much of her summers in the water. Although she was a strong swimmer, her long, heavy gown made swimming difficult. Fortunately, Audun had left her so close to the bottom that it didn't take her long to reach the ship. Seeing its resemblance to the *Sallie Mae*, she knew right away which end was the stern. With a few more powerful strokes, she reached the opening that led into the hold. Even if Ting-Tang hadn't told her which way to go, she would have figured it out from the shrill female voices.

The door that the witch doctor had described was indeed standing open. Annie didn't have to go into the room to see what was happening. Although she hadn't been sure what to expect, she was surprised to see that the two sea witches were mermaids with pale green skin and fishlike bodies from the waist down. The younger one was facing her, but her attention was focused solely on the other mermaid. Even so, Annie moved to the side so she was peering around the door and not quite so visible. *That must be Pearl*, Annie thought. With her pure white hair held back in a seed pearl band and silver eyes that flashed with anger, she was beautiful in an alluring way.

"So my creature and I aren't good enough for you?" shrieked the older mermaid. She was facing away from Annie, so it was impossible to see her face, but her hair was so fine, it was almost transparent. Wild and unrestrained, it floated around her head like something alive. Dark green scales covered her nearly as high as her neck. The skin on her arms and neck looked loose and wrinkled.

A warty creature with three long flippers and tentacles bearing leaf-shaped tips slipped off the bed that filled one corner of the room, only to ooze across the floor and out of sight. Annie shuddered. The thing had been huge and had left a sharp odor in the water. Just because she couldn't see it didn't mean that it wasn't still there.

"I suppose I was remiss in leaving you alone for so long," the sea witch continued. "I should have hunted you down ages ago. My, my, you've amassed quite a collection here. Golden sea cucumbers. The beak of a giant squid. And what's in this box? Is that my giant pearl? How did it get here? I thought that witch took it and ... Wait, that was you, wasn't it! You kept it when you knew you were supposed to give it to me! And then you ran off and took it with you. I should have guessed, you sneaky little ..."

"Put that down, Mother!" cried Pearl.

When Annie swam closer, she could see the blue and green scales that rose as high as Pearl's waist and the white seashells and sea foam that clothed her upper body.

Pointing her finger at her mother, the young sea witch sent a jet of boiling water at the older witch, making her drop the melon-size pearl back into the box. Nastia Nautica shrieked and sent a waterspout at her daughter, hurling a bench and a table against the wall and twirling Pearl around so that her seed pearl band flew off and her long hair wrapped around her throat, choking her. Pearl's face was turning a darker green when she dug her fingers into her hair and moved her lips. Suddenly her hair was loose again and Pearl was hurling spears of ice at her mother. Annie jumped back when one hit the wall near the door where she was standing.

Bubbles sprang up between the two witches, making it impossible to see. The bubbles burst when Pearl called sand in through the gaps in the walls, whipping it at her mother in a stinging, scouring cloud that made the older witch fling one arm in front of her face while pointing with the other. The cloud melted away as an oily black liquid rushed through the opening of a porthole long gone, coating Pearl from head to tail-tip.

Annie was afraid to watch when the sea witches raised their hands and pointed their fingers at each other at the same time. She had no idea what they intended, but when their power collided in the middle of the room, the resulting *BOOM!* was enough to blast Annie back down the corridor away from the door.

Annie shook her head and rubbed her ears, partly deafened by the sound. When she was sure she was all right and could hear somewhat again, she swam back to the doorway and peered inside.

The furniture was back in place and the two witches were facing each other as if their fight had never happened.

"Mother! What are you doing here? I left you on the other side of the world!"

"Look at you, Pearl! All grown up and ... What's this? A scrying bowl ... A magic mirror ... Body parts in bottles on the shelves ... You have witches' tools? Have you finally taken up the family craft?"

Pearl's voice shook when she said, "You wouldn't let me go to school with the other girls, so it's all I'm suited for, Mother. I've been studying on my own and have learned quite a lot. What's that you brought with you? You let it get on my bed? Why would you bring such a disgusting beast into my home?" Annie glanced at the bed and saw the lumpy creature watching Pearl with big, sad, puppylike eyes. The beast was enormous, but it seemed to deflate as the young sea witch's voice grew louder.

"What kind of greeting is that for your mother?" shouted Nastia Nautica. "I haven't seen you in years and the first thing you do is jump down my throat. This creature came with me from our old home. That horrid little witch Emma sent us here with her magic. Here, what's this?"

"Stop touching my belongings, Mother! This is my home, not yours. Get that beast off my bed! That animal is revolting!"

"So my creature and I aren't good enough for you? I suppose I was remiss in leaving you alone for so long. I should have hunted you down ages ago. My, my, you've amassed quite a collection here. Golden sea cucumbers. The beak of a giant squid. And what's in this box? Is that my giant pearl? How did it get here? I thought that witch took it and ... Wait, that was you, wasn't it! You kept it when you knew you were supposed to give it to me! And then you ran off and took it with you. I should have guessed, you sneaky little ..."

"Put that down, Mother!" Pointing her finger at her mother, the young sea witch sent a jet of boiling water at the older witch, making her drop the melon-size pearl back into the box.

This is it! thought Annie. *This is what Ting-Tang meant when he said that I would know when the time was right!* While Nastia Nautica sent the waterspout at her daughter, Annie crept into the room. She was reaching for the box holding the giant pearl when Pearl started hurling spears of ice at her mother. Annie ducked and one of the spears flew overhead, slamming into the wall.

Seeing the bubbles start to fill the room, Annie lurched forward and grabbed the box. She was turning to leave when the driving sand started to make the bubbles pop and she spotted a small blue bowl. Remembering that Ting-Tang had asked for a blue bowl, she grabbed it as well and hurried out of the room as the oily liquid started to turn everything dark. After stuffing the box and the bowl into the sack that Ting-Tang had given her, Annie swam as fast as she could down the corridor toward the opening at the end. She was almost there when suddenly the squishy, warty creature was in front of her, blocking her way. Annie had to back up as the creature started swimming toward her. Frantic, she was looking around for another way out when the power of the two sea witches collided and the resulting *BOOM!* blew her down the corridor and into the body of the terrifying creature.

Annie spluttered and flailed her arms and legs. She felt as if she'd been dropped into an enormous bowl of thick, viscous jelly, but it was jelly that was alive and didn't want her in it any more than she wanted to be there. With nothing solid to push against, she was beginning to panic when the creature contorted itself, pushing her out with a loud *ploop!* As soon as it was free of Annie, the creature started to swim away, undulating through the water.

Remembering Ting-Tang's warning to hurry, Annie swam out of the hold and started toward the surface.

 146

She was only partway there when a dark shape emerged from the murky water, heading straight at her.

Annie put every bit of strength into her arms and legs, trying to propel herself to the surface, but the shape was far faster. And then it was close enough that she could see Audun the dragon carrying Liam on his back. With a cry of relief, Annie darted toward them, hugging Audun's neck, then lunging at Liam and nearly knocking him off the dragon. Liam had been holding his breath, and he gasped now, as much from the hug as the amulet's magic.

"I'm so glad to see you!" she cried. "Let's get out of here. Pearl is going to notice that the giant pearl is gone any second now." Audun nodded even as he turned around. And then, with the power of a dragon beneath her and Liam's arms around her, Annie finally shot to the surface.

CHAPTER 13

THE MOMENT AUDUN REACHED the shore, Liam slipped off his back and helped Annie down. Audun hurried over to his wife, who was sitting on the beach, moaning. "Are you all right?" he asked.

"She will be as soon as she takes more of that potion I gave her," said Ting-Tang. "I told her she needed to rest. Why don't you escort her back to my camp so she can take the potion? We'll meet you there in a little while."

"That's a good idea," Audun told Millie. "Climb on my back, sweetheart. I'll have you there in two shakes of a dragon's tail."

Bending down in front of her so that his chest touched the ground, he waited for Millie to climb on and get settled. He walked carefully so as not to jostle her until he had room to spread his wings. A moment later he was airborne and circling around until he was headed back to Ting-Tang's huts.

"Dragons!" said Ting-Tang. "Who would have thought?"

"I got your blue bowl," Annie told him. "It was right by the pearl, so I grabbed them both."

"How did it go? Did you have any trouble?"

"Not until I was leaving. Nastia Nautica had some sort of squishy beast with her. It got in my way as I was swimming out of the ship. When Nastia Nautica's and Pearl's magic hit and blew up, the power of it threw me into the beast. Talk about disgusting! But I don't think it was mean or anything, and it had the sweetest eyes, sort of like Edda's."

"Who's Edda?" asked Ting-Tang.

"My dog," Annie said, liking the sound of it. She didn't know when she'd decided to keep her, just that she wasn't going to give her up. Edda was the first dog she'd ever had, and she realized that she really missed her. However, thinking about Edda reminded Annie of her father and uncle and the whole reason she was there. "I have the pearl, so now I need pure water. Do you know where I can find some?"

"The spring near my camp has the purest water I've ever found," said Ting-Tang. "It's why I built my camp there. We'll head back now. It's going to be dark in a few hours."

"Did the sea witches notice you?" Liam asked her as they started walking.

Annie shook her head. "No, but Nastia Nautica's

beast did. I don't know how intelligent it is, or if she can communicate with it, but it knows I was in the ship."

"I wonder if sea witches can come on land," said Liam.

"They're mermaids, so I doubt it, although if they're witches, who knows what they can do," replied Annie. "I just want to get this potion made and go home. I wonder where Clarence is."

"Audun will find him if anyone can," said Liam.

"I might be able to help with that," Ting-Tang told them. "That blue bowl is my scrying bowl. When we get back to my camp, I can look into the bowl and see if I can find Clarence. You'll need to ask Audun to fetch him back, though."

"I don't think he'll mind," said Annie. "He was ready to do it earlier."

They walked only a little farther before Annie turned to Liam and asked, "Why did you come after me? You weren't able to breathe underwater without the amulet. If you hadn't found me when you did, you might have drowned!"

"I knew I'd find you," said Liam. "And I couldn't leave you by yourself. When I saw that Audun had come back without you, I insisted that he take me to you. You mean everything to me, Annie. I should never have let you go without me!"

Annie went willingly when he pulled her into his arms and kissed her. The sounds of the jungle seemed to fade away until Ting-Tang said, "It's going to be dark soon and I have no desire to tromp around in the jungle at night. Are you coming with me?"

Liam pulled back from Annie enough to look into her eyes and say, "We'll continue this conversation later."

Annie smiled up at him and nodded. This was a conversation that would never grow old.

The shadows were getting long and the gloom was deepening when they finally reached Ting-Tang's camp. Annie was about to check on Millie when Ting-Tang said, "I'll get my water jug and we'll fetch the pure water you need. Bring the sack with you. We're going to need the pearl and the bowl."

Annie followed him to the hut, where he collected a large clay jug and left Chee Chee happily munching a juicy piece of fruit. Rounding the hut, they walked only a dozen paces to a pool of water that fed a small stream. "This spring flows all year long," said Ting-Tang. "It's the best-tasting water you'll find anywhere. One jugful should be enough for what both of us need tonight."

Ting-Tang knelt at the edge of the pool and half submerged the jug. While water gurgled into the clay container, Annie raised her head and looked around. It was nearly dark and the sounds were different now as some animals prepared to sleep and others to hunt. Something shrieked deeper in the jungle, making Annie wonder what might be out there, watching them. She glanced back to the huts, outlined in the fire that Audun and Liam were feeding from Ting-Tang's woodpile. The light drew her, making her wish that the witch doctor would hurry. Ting-Tang was right. The jungle was no place to be at night.

Annie was relieved to follow Ting-Tang back to the fire and the company of Liam and her friends. She took a seat beside Millie while the witch doctor poured half the jug into a large copper pot, which he then hung on a hook above the fire. "Now for the pearl," he said, holding out his hand to Annie.

Reaching into the bag, Annie pulled out the box containing the pearl. She had yet to get a really good look at it. When she held the pearl up to the firelight, she and her friends all exclaimed over its beauty.

The giant pearl was lovely. Although it was the size of a large melon, it was as perfect as its smaller cousins. Not quite white, not quite cream, it had a luster that made you want to hold it and never let it go.

"It looks like an angel rolled moonlight into a ball and sealed it with a kiss," whispered Liam.

"I've never heard you say anything like that before," Annie told him.

"That *was* really cheesy," said Audun.

"I could hold it for you," Liam said, reaching for the pearl.

"He must be under the influence already," Ting-Tang said. "Give the pearl to me." Taking it from Annie, he set it into the nearly boiling water. "Because you're immune to magic, it won't do anything to you, Annie. Millie and Audun will be fine, too, because they're dragons. But no one else should look at the pearl for more than a second or two. And make sure no one else touches it. That means you, Liam. Pearls like this one have a lot of power, and it can do things to your mind. That's why Annie should return it to the sea monster that Millie's mother stole it from. In the wrong hands, the pearl could be very dangerous."

"I know where the monster lives, or at least where it lived before Mother took its pearl. It's near the island where the witches made their home," Millie said.

"We've visited that island!" said Liam. "We know how to get there, too."

"Mother said that the monster used to live in a gap in a huge coral reef near the island. The reef is just past Nastia Nautica's shipwreck. The monster should still be somewhere around there," Millie told them. "The creature is huge. It has short arms and a pronged tail. Mother said it has a tall fin on its back, too. Oh, and my parents had to go into its mouth and back through its throat to get the pearl. They didn't realize they were inside the monster until they were trying to leave. At first they thought it was just a cave."

"We have to go inside the monster?" said Annie. "I don't know about this."

"Ah, good; a roiling boil," said Ting-Tang. "We let it do

153

that for an hour and we'll be all set. Now we can look for Clarence. I'll need that blue bowl, Annie."

Annie pulled it from the sack and handed it to Ting-Tang.

"Very good! We'll fill it about halfway," he said, pouring water into it from the jug. "And wait for the water to grow still. There, that should do it. Please be quiet, everyone. I need to concentrate."

They all watched as Ting-Tang leaned over the bowl. An image formed on the surface of the water, but Annie couldn't see it well enough to tell what it showed. When the witch doctor grunted and sat back, he rubbed his eyes as if they were tired.

"He's on a ship that's under sail," said Ting-Tang. "Are you familiar with a ship called the *Sallie Mae*? She's heading across the ocean as we speak."

"That's the ship we came on!" said Annie. "He stole our ride home!"

"Not for long," Audun announced. "I'll find it and bring it back."

"Would you like your supper first?" asked Millie.

"No, thank you, love," said Audun. "I'll catch some fish on my way."

"Uh, I wasn't planning to feed so many people," said Ting-Tang. "I thought you'd leave as soon as you had the potion. I really don't have enough food."

"We'd love to leave, but we can't go without our ship," said Annie.

Audun sighed. "If it's not one thing, it's another. I'll be right back with something for supper." He took off into the air with a whoosh of wings that blew the flames into a wild dance and made the trees bend and sway.

"Where did he go?" asked Ting-Tang.

"Hunting probably," said Liam.

Millie got to her feet, looking shaky. "I'm going to lie down for a while. Please wake me when you're ready to leave."

"Are you all right?" asked Annie.

Millie nodded. "I will be. Ting-Tang's potion should start working soon."

Liam sat down beside Annie, adding sticks to the fire now and then, while Annie and Ting-Tang kept an eye on the boiling water. "You told us why you left Treecrest," Annie said to Ting-Tang after a while, "but have you ever thought about going back? I'm sure you'd be treated with respect now. You're very good at what you do and you'd have as many patients as you were willing to take on. Most of the doctors who came to treat my father were fools, and the herbalists had no idea how to handle something as serious as the creeping blue. We could really use someone like you in our part of the world."

"I hadn't really thought about it," the witch doctor replied.

"You might want to consider it," said Annie. "You'll always be welcome in Treecrest. I'll make sure there is a place for you."

"Or you could come to Dorinocco," said Liam. "You could live in the castle if you'd like. We could use a good royal physician like you."

Ting-Tang shrugged. "Maybe someday, when I get tired of living in paradise. Thank you for the offer. I'll keep it in mind."

All three of them looked up when the foliage rustled and a dark shape descended from the sky. Audun strode toward the fire with a large fish clamped between his jaws. It was a big fish, at least twelve feet long, and it wore a swordlike fixture attached to the front of its head.

"A swordfish!" exclaimed Ting-Tang. "I love swordfish steaks!"

The fish was still alive and it flopped from side to side when Audun dropped it on the ground. Annie backed away from the heaving fish and its nasty-looking sword. "It's awfully big," she said.

"Biggest I've ever seen!" Ting-Tang said, rubbing his hands together. "I usually ask for some sort of payment for my potions, but this fish takes care of that! Plus you rescued me, which counts for a lot. This fish is something else, though! We'll have steaks tonight and I'll start smoking the rest in the morning."

"Is Millie all right?" Audun asked, looking around for his wife.

"She's lying down in the hut," Annie told him.

"I want to get her home as soon as I can," said Audun.

"I'll go fetch Clarence. I should be back by morning, if not before."

"The pearl has steeped long enough," said Ting-Tang. Slipping a glove made of woven grasses on his hand, he poured the water from the pot into a bottle. After shoving a cork in the bottle, he handed the potion and a silver thimble to Annie.

"Give each patient a thimbleful of the potion. You should see results right away. There's enough in that bottle to last for many generations, although you probably only need it for one or two more. The Blue Death, or creeping blue, as you call it, is hereditary, but never lasts more than a few generations. Be sure to keep that potion somewhere safe."

"Oh, I will!" said Annie.

"We have to let the pearl cool before we put it back in the box," said Ting-Tang. "But it looks as if you're going to spend the night here anyway." He glanced at the swordfish, which was no longer moving. "Tell me, who wants a swordfish steak?"

꩜

Audun returned shortly before dawn the next morning. Although Annie and Liam had intended to wait up for him, they had finally gone to sleep in one of the patient huts. Annie woke enough to hear Liam's and Clarence's voices, but not enough to actually get up. She woke again a few hours later to the sound of Clarence shouting.

"I'm not staying here!" he cried as Annie left the hut. "What am I supposed to do, weave grass mats all day?"

Annie noticed that he was bound hand and foot again. She thought it was a good idea, considering everything he'd done.

"I wasn't asking what *you* wanted," Liam told him. "I want to hear what Ting-Tang has to say. Is it all right if my brother stays here with you? He can be your assistant or whatever you need."

"I don't really need an assistant," said Ting-Tang. "Although it would help if someone fished and set snares for food. Picking fruit would be good, too. And maybe clean the huts after my patients leave. Then I could spend more time on my studies. I guess I could use some help after all. Sure, your brother can stay."

"If you decide to come back to Treecrest or go someplace with people around, please take him somewhere he can't escape," said Annie. "We don't want him ever coming home again. All he does is cause big trouble when he's there. He's tried to take over Treecrest twice."

"I promise," said Ting-Tang. "I left Treecrest because it wasn't right for me at the time, but my family still lives there and I'm fond of the kingdom. Now you've given me real incentive to keep Clarence here."

"One other thing," said Liam. "Please don't untie him until a few hours after we leave for the beach, just to make sure he can't follow us."

"I won't," said Ting-Tang. "He can sit right here with

me while I smoke the swordfish. We'll be eating sword-fish steaks for months!"

"Please take me with you!" Clarence cried to his brother. "I don't even like fish!"

"You lost any hope of gaining my sympathy long ago," said Liam. "Maybe this experience will help you learn how to be a decent person."

"You think you're so great!" Clarence shouted, his face turning red. "But you're nothing! Mother was right!"

"Let's go, Annie," said Liam. "Thank you for every-thing, Ting-Tang. Don't be afraid to make Clarence work for his keep."

"Oh, I won't," said Ting-Tang. "I'm starting a list. I keep thinking of more things he can do!"

The others had to raise their voices to be heard over Clarence's shouting, but they all thanked the witch doctor and said good-bye as they started into the jun-gle. Audun had stayed a dragon, so he went first, swish-ing his tail back and forth to widen the path that Liam, Millie, and Clarence had used the day before. The birds flew away as they approached and if there were any animals in the underbrush, they stayed hidden.

༜

The *Sallie Mae* was anchored in the cove just where they'd left it when they'd disembarked. The captain was wait-ing for them at the railing when they boarded the ship. "I'm so sorry!" he said, bowing to Liam. "Your brother came on board and convinced me that savages had killed you all. If I'd known that he was lying, we never would have left you behind."

"I understand," said Liam. "Clarence can be very convincing. He mastered the art of lying long ago."

"We're really happy that you're still alive," said one of the sailors. "No one on the ship likes Prince Clarence. You should have seen his face when Master Audun showed up as a dragon! The prince screamed and hid in the galley."

"He was sure they didn't exist," said Annie. "It must have been a shock to finally learn that there really are dragons."

CHAPTER 14

ANNIE STOOD ON the deck with Liam until they could no longer see the shoreline. While he stayed to talk to the captain, she went below to their cabin to put the bottle with the potion and the box containing the pearl in her luggage. She was trying to get the snarls out of her hair when the ship stopped with a sudden lurch, tossing her halfway across the cabin. For a moment, the ship was silent except for the sound of the waves smacking against the hull. And then the voices started, some from the other cabins, but most above deck. Some of the voices were angry, some were frightened, some demanded answers. Getting to her feet, Annie tossed her brush onto the bed and hurried out the door. Audun, a human again, was already pounding up the stairs with Millie close behind. Annie ran after them and reached the deck just as Liam shouted, "Who are you and what do you want?"

Liam and the captain were standing by the railing, facing something Annie couldn't see. It wasn't until she'd joined them at the railing that she saw a figure riding the crest of a stationary wave only a few yards from the ship. At first Annie had no idea who it was, but then she saw the nearly translucent hair and the dark green scales and realized that Nastia Nautica had found her.

For the first time Annie was able to see the sea witch's face. Although the skin on her neck and arms was loose and wrinkled like an older lady's, the skin on her face was as taut as the heads of Ting-Tang's drums. Her lips were thin and her nose was narrow and pointed, but her eyes were her most arresting features. Two black circles stared at the people on board the ship, turning to Annie as she drew closer. Annie had never seen anyone without whites in their eyes, and she thought they were highly disturbing.

"There she is!" screeched Nastia Nautica. "That's the thief who stole my pearl!"

When Liam glanced behind him and saw Annie, he moved so that he was between his wife and the sea witch. Annie stepped around him so that she was facing Nastia Nautica again. "This is my fight, not yours," she murmured to her husband.

"You're my wife, so it's mine as well," he replied, taking her hand.

"Give me back my pearl!" the sea witch screamed. With a twitch of her hand, the wave that was supporting her rose another ten feet into the air so that she was looking down on everyone.

"I'm not giving you anything!" Annie called back.

"I'd reconsider if I were you!" cried the sea witch. "You either hand over the pearl, or I'll have my beast take your ship apart board by board until I find the pearl myself!"

The witch wiggled her fingers and something big and wet slapped against the hull. Translucent tendrils slurped over the railing, hauling Nastia Nautica's creature onto the deck. It fell on the wooden planks with a loud *sploosh!* "You can't do this, Mother!" Pearl cried, rising up on a wave of her own. "Someone like you should never have that pearl. I took it from you because I knew you'd use it for something evil and nasty. If anyone should have the pearl, it's me!"

"And what would you do with it—put it in your jewelry chest and wear it on fancy occasions?" Nastia Nautica said with a sneer.

"I'd keep it safe from people like you!" Pearl shouted at her mother. With a swoosh of her hand, she made the column of water supporting Nastia Nautica lose its shape and fall back into the sea.

"How dare you!" her mother screeched. Drawing water from the depths of the ocean, she sent a huge

wave crashing over Pearl's head, nearly capsizing the *Sallie Mae.*

The ship tilted until the floor was nearly vertical. The people scrambled to stay on board, grabbing hold of whatever they could reach. Liam snagged Annie with one hand while wrapping his free arm around the mast. Annie caught hold of a sailor as he fell past her, nearly dislocating her shoulder as his weight swung her around.

When the ship rocked back in the opposite direction, it didn't tilt as far. It soon began to level out and Annie began to look around. She was surprised to see that Nastia Nautica's creature had stretched itself between a mast and a railing, and that three sailors were embedded in its squishy body. As the water around the ship grew calmer, the creature twisted itself, squirting the men out of its body like seeds from an orange.

"That was the most disgusting thing that's ever happened to me!" one of the sailors said as he wiped slime off his face.

Annie frowned and turned to the man. "At least you didn't fall off the ship and drown," she told him.

While the ship's crew ran around trying to make sure everyone was all right and set everything back where it was supposed to go, Annie glanced at the sea witches. Nastia Nautica was motioning with her hands, trying to enclose her daughter in an oily-looking ball of water,

even while Pearl was sending small jellyfish to plaster themselves all over her mother. They were so involved in fighting each other that neither one was looking at the people on the ship. Hoping that Nastia Nautica and Pearl would stay busy for a while, Annie hurried to the creature that was halfheartedly trying to pull a plank out of the decking.

"I know you aren't mean or nasty like Nastia Nautica," Annie began. "And I'm sure you don't really want to do this. You don't seem to be happy with the sea witch, so I don't know why you stay with her."

The creature turned its sorrowful gaze on Annie even as it stopped pulling on the planking.

"Now is your chance to get away," Annie told it. "You could flee while Nastia Nautica and Pearl are fighting. Nastia Nautica won't notice if you leave this very minute. Go now and swim as fast as you can so she can't find you."

The beast stared at her for a moment, then began to slide backward toward the railing opposite from where the witches were fighting. Oozing over the side of the ship, it disappeared, hitting the water with a loud *plop!* Annie ran to the railing to watch the creature undulate out of sight.

When Annie turned back to the two sea witches, most of the jellyfish were gone and Pearl was trying to pry starfish off her face. Nastia Nautica was chortling with glee and pitching more starfish at her daughter when Annie joined her friends at the railing. "What are we going to do if Nastia Nautica wins?" Annie asked them.

"If it looks as if that's going to happen, I can turn into my dragon self and make the water around her boil," said Millie.

Audun leaned over to kiss his wife on the cheek. "That won't be necessary." Turning back to the sea witches, he shouted, "Nastia Nautica! Remember me?"

The older sea witch looked up from hurling starfish. "No, why should I?"

"Maybe you'll remember me better if I look like this!" Audun replied as the air around him began to shimmer. A moment later, Audun the dragon was there, already spreading his wings.

Nastia Nautica recognized him then. Her face twisted in rage and she began to scream, "It's you! You're the one who stole my flute! You took the desicca bird from me when it hadn't finished its job. And it was you who rescued that horrid witch Emma! Why, if I—"

Audun didn't give the sea witch a chance to finish her threat. She was still ranting at him when he took to the air and swooped down. The witch had scarcely raised her hand to point at him when he plucked her from the sea, pinning her arms and hands to her sides. Even Annie had seen enough to know that the sea witch needed to gesture to make her magic work, so she wasn't surprised when all Nastia Nautica could do was kick and scream. Lifting the sea witch high into the air, Audun carried her toward the shore, disappearing over the jungle.

As the water around the ship grew calm, everyone watched as Pearl pulled the last few starfish off her face. She was tossing them into the water when Audun came back without Nastia Nautica.

"What did you do with her?" Liam asked as Audun landed on the deck.

"I dropped her into the pool in the bottom of the pit where we found Ting-Tang," Audun replied.

"You know that pool might open into underground caves," said Liam. "Eventually she might be able to make her way back to the sea."

"I know," Audun told him. "But by then we'll be long gone."

"Can mermaids survive in freshwater?" asked Millie.

"I have no idea," said Audun.

"It will make her ill, but she'll survive," Pearl replied before turning to Annie. The young sea witch had called up a wave to hold her level with the deck and face-to-face with Annie and her friends. "I need to ask you, what do you intend to do with the giant pearl?"

"Return it to the sea monster that owned it before Millie's mother took it, unless you have a better idea," said Annie.

Pearl laughed. "The sea monster didn't just own it. The monster created it. That pearl didn't come from

167

any oyster. It may look like a pearl, but it's actually something very different. Everyone just calls it a pearl for lack of a better name. Now that I think about it, I believe that your proposal is an excellent solution. The monster can probably keep it safer than anyone else. I was going to take the pearl back from you, but instead I believe I'll let you complete your task. Just make sure you keep it safe until you give it to the monster. It's too dangerous to let it fall into the wrong hands."

"I'll guard it with my life," said Annie. "But do we have to put it back exactly where it was before? I really dread the idea of going into the monster's mouth and down its gullet."

"Throat," said Millie.

"Either way," Annie went on. "Couldn't we just fling the pearl at the monster and leave?"

"That sounds like a much better plan," Liam said.

Pearl shook her head. "You have to get it in the monster's mouth at least. Otherwise the pearl might lie on the sea floor unnoticed until someone bad comes along."

"I know the monster was last seen near the witches' island, but where should we look exactly?" asked Liam.

"If you're on the witches' beach, enter the water and go straight ahead for four hundred yards, then turn left," Pearl told him. "After you've gone another hundred yards, you should see Coral's castle. There's a seaweed forest behind it. Go through the forest and you'll see the shipwreck where my mother used to live. The monster lived in a coral reef near there, but it could be anywhere by now."

"It sounds awfully complicated," said Annie.

"We can handle it," said Liam. "You know, Annie, we might as well be the ones to take it. We were going there anyway. Do you mind if we borrow your amulet, Audun? I don't know how we'll do this otherwise."

"Of course you can," said Audun. "Next time we need it, we'll just come see you. It will give Millie and me a good reason to visit."

"If that's all settled, I'll be off," said Pearl. "My mother knows where I live now, so it's time for me to move. It's too bad. I really do like that ship. Ah well, at least I got to stay there as long as I did. Good-bye, everyone." With a wave of her hand and a flick of her tail, the mermaid sea witch disappeared back into the water.

"What did you mean when you said that we were going there anyway?" Annie asked Liam. "Where are we going, the monster's coral reef?"

"Close enough," said Liam. "After we take the potion to Treecrest, we're going to visit the island where the witches live. It would be the perfect place for my mother. She's always liked witches, and it's far enough away."

"I'm glad you finally made a decision about her," replied Annie.

"So am I!" Liam said. "Now I can't wait to leave her there

so we never have to see her again. All we'll have to do is convince the witches to keep her there."

"And I can't wait to take this potion to my father and Uncle Rupert," said Annie. "This already took far too long!"

CHAPTER 15

THE TRIP BACK to Kenless wasn't nearly as long as the hunt for Skull Cove. Rather than looking for islands or following the coastline, Audun used his dragon senses to take them straight across the ocean to the seaport. When the wind died down, he used his newfound ability to control the winds to make it strong again. The *Sallie Mae* sped across the water with a tailwind filling her sails. Fortunately, they didn't encounter any more pirates, witches, or sea monsters on the trip.

Annie became more and more agitated the closer they came to shore. Now that the end of the trip was approaching, she felt guilty for having enjoyed the voyage as much as she had. While hunting for the cove and the witch doctor, she had let the search distract her from thinking about the suffering her father and uncle were enduring. With the potion in hand, their illness was all she could think about. Too upset to stand still, she paced back and forth across the deck as if that would help them go faster. The others stood by the railing, looking up every time she walked past.

After watching Annie for a while, Millie turned to her husband. "Audun, do you think the captain knows the way to port from here?"

Audun shrugged. "All he has to do is go straight ahead. At this rate we'll be there in about two hours."

"Then why don't you carry Annie to her parents' castle? Liam and I can stay on the ship until we reach the port, then take the carriage back. The sooner Annie gets the potion to her family, the sooner her father and uncle will be cured and she can stop worrying."

"I don't like leaving you behind," said Audun.

"I'll be fine," Millie told him. "Liam will take care of me, won't you, Liam?"

"Of course," he replied. "I wouldn't let anything happen to Millie, and I know it would mean a lot to Annie."

"If you're sure . . . ," Audun said to his wife.

"Absolutely!" said Millie.

Audun kissed her on the cheek. "Then I should go talk to the captain."

"And I'll try to catch up with Annie so I can tell her!" Millie announced.

Annie was in the bow of the ship, gazing toward the still invisible land, when Millie found her. "Go get the potion. I have a bag you can use to carry it," Millie told her. "Audun is going to fly you to Treecrest as soon as he's talked to the captain."

"What? Why? I mean, I thought we were going together," said Annie.

"Liam and I will be right behind you in the carriage," Millie said. "This way you can get the potion to your father and uncle that much faster. It's still daylight, and… Oh, I suppose that could be a problem. People aren't used to seeing dragons around here. Maybe you and Audun should wait until dark."

"Forget that!" exclaimed Annie. "There are lives at stake! Please let Audun know that I'll be ready in a few minutes."

Annie ran below deck to get the potion. When she returned a few minutes later, she was carrying the potion and the box containing the pearl. Both Audun and Liam had joined Millie, and they all looked at the wooden box when she appeared. "You're taking that with you, too?" asked Millie.

"I have to," said Annie. "Pearl said to keep it safe."

"I don't think it will fit even if we take it out of the box," Millie said, studying the bag she'd brought.

"But I have to take the pearl!" said Annie. "I don't dare leave it with the luggage. Someone might take it, and you heard what Ting-Tang said about how dangerous it is!"

"I can carry it for you," said Audun. "It won't affect me and it should fit in my pouch. I can't fit that box, though."

"I don't need the box," said Annie, taking out the pearl.

"Here, give me the potion," Millie said, taking it from Annie. "It can go in this bag. I thought we could strap it to your back so you don't drop it."

When Annie glanced at Audun, he had already turned into a dragon. "That was fast," Annie said, handing him the pearl. She watched while he raised his wing and tucked the pearl into a pouch made from loose skin. The skin drew tight when he lowered his wing, so she wasn't worried that it would fall out.

Once Millie had helped Annie strap the bag containing the potion to her back, Annie was ready to go. "Millie and I will ride in the carriage all night," Liam told his wife. "We should reach the castle by midafternoon." He kissed her then, making her wish that she weren't in such a hurry.

It was early evening when Annie finally climbed onto Audun's back. Even as she waved good-bye to Liam and Millie, her thoughts were already turning to the invalids at home, worried that she might not get the potion there in time.

"Hold on tight," Audun told her. "I'm going to fly high so no one will see us as more than a speck in the sky. We can go lower once the sun sets."

Annie bent over Audun's neck as he angled upward, wrapping her arms around him as far as they would go. She could feel the temperature of the air change the higher they went, and soon began to wish she'd worn something warmer. When Audun leveled off, they were high above the sparse clouds, and Annie forgot about being cold. She felt like she could see forever, and she marveled at how small everything below her appeared. There was the ocean with the port just ahead. The miniature town around it looked like a child's toy set; the people were too small to see. The patchwork farmland came next, with hedgerows and stone walls dividing one section from the next. And then they were flying over the forest, a different shade of green than what she'd seen when flying over the jungle, but just as lush and beautiful.

Annie glanced to her right. The sun was setting, turning the sky pink and orange. It was glorious, but she would have enjoyed it more if it hadn't reminded her how quickly time was passing. As the sky grew dark, Annie's stomach began to hurt from worry. She had to get there in time; she just had to!

ॐ

Annie had no way of telling the time, but she was sure it was well after midnight when she spotted her parents' castle. Audun had started flying lower hours before, so they could easily see the flickering of candles in the windows of one of the rooms. "That's my uncle's chamber," Annie told Audun. "I hope this doesn't mean we're too late!"

"We'll find out in a few minutes," Audun told her. "I need to land where the sentries can't see me. I'd rather not get shot full of arrows if I can help it! Thank goodness sentries rarely look up when they aren't used to having dragons around."

Annie swallowed hard. In her concern over her father and uncle, she hadn't thought about how the guards might react when they first saw a dragon. As Audun began his descent, Annie held her breath and didn't exhale until he had safely landed in her mother's flower garden. He had scarcely closed his wings when she slid off his back and started running. A moment later, Audun, in human form, was running right behind her.

Annie headed straight for her uncle's room, racing up one flight of stairs, then down the corridor. Her heart sank when she saw people gathered outside the door, talking in low voices. She didn't slow down until she reached the room and had to squeeze between the people. The room was so crowded that she couldn't see much at first, but as she pushed forward, she spotted her mother seated beside the bed. The doctors that the family had consulted earlier were lined up behind her. Rupert must have been close to death if her mother had asked them to come back. Annie's sister, Gwendolyn, was sitting on the other side with her new husband, Prince Beldegard. Big Boy was there as well, sitting beside Gwendolyn with his great head resting on Rupert's hand.

"Is he still alive?" Annie asked as she made her way closer.

A woman gasped as if Annie had said something she shouldn't have said, but Annie didn't care. She pushed past her just as Dr. Hemshaw tried to pour liquid between Rupert's closed lips. "Whatever you're trying to give him, stop it!" Annie said as she struggled to undo the straps holding the bag on her back.

"Annie, you're here!" cried her mother.

"Thank goodness!" exclaimed Gwendolyn.

"Your sister came when she heard the news," the queen told Annie. "We've been so worried that you wouldn't get back in time."

"Well, I'm here now and everything is going to be all right. But why are all these people in the room? Get out!" Annie told the onlookers. "This isn't your evening's entertainment. This man is sick and needs some air."

Some of the people grumbled and seemed reluctant to leave, but when Annie glared at them they began to shuffle out.

"That goes for all of you, too," she told the doctors.

"I'm giving Prince Rupert tonic to ease his suffering," said Dr. Hemshaw, tilting his head so he was looking down his nose at Annie.

"I told you to get away from him!" Annie snapped. She had no time for pompous men who didn't know what they were doing. Seeing Audun approaching the

177

bed, she waved him closer. "Please escort that man from the room. I need to give my uncle the cure."

Her mother gave her a sharp glance and half rose from her seat. "You found it?"

"We found it," she said, nodding at Audun. Pulling the straps off her shoulders, Annie swung the bag in front of her and undid the string tying it closed. Her mother stood up and let Annie take her seat. Big Boy glanced at her without moving his head. The sadness in his eyes was almost overwhelming.

For the first time since she'd walked in the room, Annie was able to get a good look at her uncle. He was lying on his back, with his eyes closed, breathing heavily as if it took great effort to draw air into his lungs.

"He's in a lot of pain," murmured the queen.

Annie nodded. Her uncle was blue up to his chin, but his face was almost as pale as the moon. "Then there's no time to waste," Annie said, taking the bottle and the thimble out of the bag.

Annie poured the potion into the thimble. "Here you go," she told her uncle, holding the thimble to his lips. "I consulted a witch doctor who has treated this illness before. This is the cure. All you have to do is drink it."

Annie wasn't sure if her uncle was aware of her or what she had said when she poured the first drops between his lips. After a little had trickled in, however, his lips parted, making it easier to give him the rest.

When she saw his throat move, she knew that he had swallowed it.

Nothing happened at first, and Annie held her breath without realizing it. Suddenly, Rupert began to shake violently from head to toe. The tremors were lessening when he began to cough. Big Boy raised his head and barked, a deep *whoof!* that drowned out the sound of her uncle's coughing. When he coughed again, Dr. Hemshaw stuck his head back into the room. "That was a death rattle. Whatever you gave your uncle, you just killed him."

"I don't think so," said Annie as her uncle continued to cough. When he stopped, there was a hint of pink in his cheeks and the blue was already receding from his chin.

"Thank you, Annie," Rupert said, his voice the faintest whisper.

"You're very welcome," Annie replied, and kissed him on the cheek.

"Oh my!" cried her mother. "You did it! You actually found the cure. Oh, Rupert, I'm so glad! And your father, Annie. Your father!"

"We need to go to him!" cried Gwendolyn.

"Just a moment," said Annie. "I want to make sure it really works."

Annie smiled when Big Boy raised his head, revealing Rupert's twitching fingers. As the blue receded down Rupert's neck, he seemed to gain strength and he was able to reach up and pet the dog. Big Boy's plumed tail began to thump Gwendolyn's chair.

Annie laughed with joy. Her uncle really was going to be all right! "I'll see you in a bit, Uncle Rupert," she said before turning to her mother. "Let's go see Father now. I'll race you there!"

Gwendolyn, Beldegard, and Audun joined Annie and her mother as they reached the door. Feeling light-hearted for the first time in weeks, they ran down the hall and up a flight of stairs, laughing. Although Annie was the first one to reach the door, it was the queen who threw it open. Edda had been lying beside the king's bed, but she jumped up now and ran to greet Annie.

"What's all this?" the king grumbled from his bed.

"I'm sorry if we woke you, Father, but we brought you something that you are going to like very much," Annie said as she crossed the room with Edda at her side.

"You didn't wake me, child," her father said. "I've been lying here awake for hours. What did you bring me? If it's something to eat, I don't want it. Your mother has been after me to eat for days."

"You don't eat this, Father, you drink it. Here," Annie said, pouring the potion into the thimble. "Drink all of it and I guarantee you'll feel a lot better."

"It's the cure, Halbert!" exclaimed the queen. "Annie found the cure! Rupert was about to die and she gave him the cure and he's much better already. Will you please just drink it?"

The king grunted and looked from the queen to Annie. "The cure, is it? Now that's a story I'd like to hear. All right, hand it over. We'll see if this really works!"

Annie gave him the thimble and watched him sniff the contents. "You must drink every drop," she told him.

"It smells slightly fishy. It wasn't made from fish, was it?" he asked, giving the thimble a dubious look.

Annie shook her head. "I watched the witch doctor make the potion. He didn't use any fish."

The king sighed. "I can scarcely keep food down, and you want me to drink this. Ah well. Here goes." Tilting the thimble, he emptied it into his mouth all at once and swallowed with an audible gulp.

"Just a moment," said the queen. Taking a candle from a nearby table, she brought it closer to the king's bedside. "Where was the blue the last time you looked?" she asked.

"It had almost reached my chest," her husband replied.

"Look and see where it is now," she directed.

"So soon?" said the king. "I just drank it, and . . . Oh, I feel odd."

The king began to shake just like Rupert had when he drank the potion. When the coughing started, Annie and her mother looked at each other. Annie thought it was an encouraging sign. After an extra-loud cough, the king sighed and fell back against his pillows.

"Halbert, are you all right?" asked his wife.

"You know, I think I am," said the king. "I actually feel much better!" Lifting the neck of his nightshirt, he peered down at his stomach. "There's less blue already! Your potion is working, Annie!"

"Thank goodness!" exclaimed the queen. "I was so afraid I was going to lose you. I don't know what I would have done without you, Halbert!"

"Nor I without you, my dearest," the king said, smiling tenderly at his wife.

Annie yawned and her jaw made a cracking sound. Suddenly she was so tired that she could hardly keep her eyes open. After flying for so long on the back of a dragon, she didn't have any energy left.

"It looks as if you don't need me right now," she told her parents. "If you don't mind, I'm going to bed."

"That's a good idea," said the queen as she took a seat beside the king.

"Liam and our friend Millie should be here by midday, but Audun needs a place to sleep tonight," Annie said, and yawned again.

The queen took her husband's hand and moved a little closer to him.

"I'll have the steward see to it," said Gwendolyn. "Go to bed, Annie. You need your rest! We should go, too, Beldegard. I think my parents would like to be alone.

Good night, Father. I'm so happy that you're going to be all right!"

"Thank you, my dear," he replied. "And thank you for all you've done, Annie! I owe you my life now!" her father called as she left his chamber with Edda pressed against her leg.

"You're welcome," Annie murmured as she shut the door. She was so tired, she imagined that she heard her mother giggle.

૨૭

Annie slept in the next morning. She would have slept even later if a maid hadn't knocked on the door of her chamber. "What is it?" Annie asked, sounding groggy.

Edda had slept on the floor beside Annie's bed. The big dog got up now and padded across the room.

The maid opened the door and peeked in. "I apologize for disturbing you, Your Highness, but Queen Karolina requests your presence in the great hall. Hi, Edda. Do you want to go out?"

While Edda wagged her tail and nosed the door open wider, Annie sat up and stretched. "You can tell the queen that I'll be down as soon as I get dressed."

"Very good, Your Highness. Come on, Edda. Let's go," the maid said, letting the dog out of the room.

Annie groaned as she got out of bed. Riding a dragon was fun, but it used muscles she didn't know she had, and now every one of them ached. She would love a hot bath, if only she had the time. Instead, she hurried to get dressed and gave her hair a cursory brushing.

As she walked through the corridors, Annie wondered why they were so quiet. Could something have gone wrong? It occurred to her that the potion might not have worked as well as she'd thought, and that the improvements in her father's and uncle's conditions had been only temporary. Suddenly apprehensive, she hurried to the great hall.

She stopped worrying as she approached the hall and heard the sound of a large group of people talking and laughing. When she stepped into the doorway, she found that everyone was seated at the long tables that were usually filled only in the evenings.

"There she is!" the king called out, and everyone turned toward the door.

Annie blushed as they all cheered. When Edda trotted over and bumped against her leg, Annie placed her hand on the dog's back and walked with her to the head table.

"Your father and I were starving this morning, so we decided to have a feast," Prince Rupert said when she reached the table. "It's really in your honor, though. We can't thank you enough for finding the cure. I was sure I was about to die last night, and your father wouldn't have lasted much longer."

Annie smiled at her uncle. He looked better than she had ever seen him, with color in his cheeks, a sparkle in his eyes, and the erect posture of a military man. Big Boy was lying at his feet, asleep. If even the dog wasn't worried, Rupert had to be all right!

An empty seat waited between her uncle and Audun. As Annie sat down, her father leaned forward to look past her friend and say, "Thank you again, Annie. Not one of those idiots who came to treat us knew what to do. I'd like to meet that witch doctor you mentioned. At least *he* knows his trade."

"He does," said Annie. "I invited him to come to Treecrest. He said he would consider it."

Annie noticed that the doctors who had tried to treat her father were seated at a table near enough to hear her. A few of the doctors looked interested, but Dr. Hemshaw just scowled and took a sip from his tankard.

"We had hoped that Liam and Millie would be here in time to join us, but they haven't arrived yet," said the queen.

"I'm sure they'll be here soon," said Audun.

Annie gave him a closer look. Although everyone else seemed satisfied with his answer, she knew him well enough by now to tell that he was worried. True, he seemed to worry about Millie a lot, but Annie hoped that this time he wasn't justified.

Sitting back, Annie helped herself from a passing platter. She noticed how healthy her father looked, and that both men ate hearty amounts of the feast the cooks had prepared. Although she was delighted to see them like this, as time passed, and people finished eating, Annie began to worry, too. Liam and Millie should have reached the castle by now. She knew that something as simple as a lame horse or broken wheel might have held them up, but she couldn't help but think that it might be something far more serious.

As the feast ended and her family began to get up from the table, Annie turned to Audun. "Millie and Liam aren't back yet. I think we should go look for them."

"I was thinking the same thing," he replied. "You know I can't ride a horse, and a carriage wouldn't be fast enough."

"Then we're going to have to fly, aren't we?" said Annie. "We can stay high up like we did before, but what if they're in the forest? How will we see them through the trees?"

"We won't need to see them," Audun told her. "I'd recognize Millie's scent anywhere."

"Then let's go," said Annie. "We've waited long enough."

CHAPTER 16

No one questioned them when Annie and Audun went for a walk along the riverbank soon after the feast. They left through the gate facing the forest and headed for the water in case someone was watching. The moment they were out of sight and were sure no one could see them, Audun turned into a dragon and crouched down. Without Liam's help, it was hard for Annie to climb onto Audun's scaly back, but when she faltered, the dragon helped by turning his head and giving her a push with his nose.

Annie had worn warmer clothes this time, so she was prepared when they rose into the sky and kept climbing. They didn't go quite as high as they had before; just enough that people would think Audun was a large bird if they happened to look up. When Audun was satisfied that he was high enough, he turned to fly over the road, and they both peered down, hoping to see the carriage and the guards. They flew back the way they had come the night before, passing above farmland, forest, stone houses, and straw huts. Neither Annie nor Audun saw any sign of the carriage or the guards. Audun kept sniffing for Millie's scent, but all he could find was her trail from their trip to Kenless.

They were well south of the castle when Audun finally turned his head to Annie and said, "I've found Millie's scent. Hold on tight!"

Annie wrapped her arms more tightly around the dragon's neck when he pressed his wings to his sides and dropped like a stone. The wind whistled around them as they plummeted straight down toward the forest, pulling up at the last moment to skim the tops of the trees. The leaves were so thick that Annie couldn't see the road, but Audun seemed to know right where to go. Reaching a gap in the branches, he slipped between the trees, landing in the middle of the road. Annie would have been relieved to see the royal carriage of Treecrest if she hadn't noticed the fighting first. A tree was down in front of the carriage, which had forced the driver to stop. Bandits were attacking the guards, trying to reach the carriage. Using curved cutlasses, they slashed at the sword-wielding guards, moving back and forth across the road as they advanced and retreated. The combatants seemed to be evenly matched, because as far as Annie could tell, no one was winning.

"I see Liam," Audun declared. "Millie must still be in the carriage. I know you don't want people to see me like this, but I'm a much more effective fighter as a dragon. Would you mind terribly if I engaged the bandits while I was in this form?"

Annie spotted Liam now. While guards fought bandits all around the carriage, Liam stood in front of the carriage door, protecting it from four bandits at once. He was badly outnumbered, and if he didn't get help soon, he was bound to tire and make a mistake.

"Go for it!" Annie told Audun, clambering off his back. She no longer cared if people saw the dragons. The pirates had already seen them, which meant word was bound to get out if it hadn't already. As far as Annie was concerned, having a dragon on their side was a definite advantage.

"Stay here," Audun said as gas began to trickle from his nostrils. "I don't want my breath to hurt you."

"And I don't want to get in your way," Annie said, stepping aside. "You do whatever you need to do to end this now!"

The door to the carriage started to open. Liam noticed and shouted, "Don't come out!" even as he avoided the swipes of two cutlasses at once. The bandits rushed forward, only to have Liam beat them back. One of the bandits was bigger than the others and particularly vicious in his attack, wielding his cutlass like an expert. Annie stepped to the side, trying to get a better look. When she saw his bald head and full beard, she realized that he was the pirate captain Prickly Beard.

A sudden breeze ruffled Annie's hair and the hem of her gown. Audun had taken to the air. Rising just above the fighting men, he fanned his wings and ROARED! That got everyone's attention. The guards had never seen the dragon before. Although they looked frightened, they stood their ground and a few even raised their swords as if they were willing to fight him. The bandits, however, didn't look nearly as brave.

"It's the dragon!" shouted the man Captain Riley had called Short Jack.

"You said that if it hadn't come before this, it wasn't going to show up!" a man with bare feet and oddly shaped toes shouted at the captain. "I should have stayed with Slippery Pete!"

When Audun roared again, the bandits turned and ran.

Annie hurried to Liam's side while Audun chased the bandits into the forest. "Are you all right?" she cried.

"I am now!" he said, putting his arm around her. "Those bandits have been plaguing us all day."

"May I come out?" Millie asked, opening the carriage door.

"Of course," said Liam as he moved out of the way.

"Your husband wouldn't let me get involved," Millie

said to Annie. "I told him that chasing off the bandits was worth an upset stomach, but he made me promise not to turn into my dragon self unless things got bad."

"Thank you for that!" Audun said, landing beside the carriage.

"And thank you for coming by when you did," Liam told him. "We would have reached the castle hours ago if the bandits hadn't sent men ahead to cut down trees and delay us. My men and I had to cut up two other downed trees today. It's why you should always keep an ax or two under the carriage seat. A tree lying across the road is a bandit's favorite way to stop a carriage."

"They were persistent!" declared Audun.

Liam nodded. "We rode all night without any problems and came across the first tree just after dawn. The bandits must have thought it would hold us for a while, but it didn't take us long to clear the road. They must have planned this ahead of time and had men ready to chop down more trees if the first one didn't work. The main group of them didn't catch up until just a little while ago. I don't know what they thought we had, but they were very determined to get it."

"They weren't just bandits," said Annie. "They were the pirates who attacked the *Sallie Mae*. From what Snaggle Toes said, I think they stopped you the first two times to see if Audun would show up. When he didn't, they thought it was safe to attack you."

191

"I don't understand why they were so determined to stop the carriage," Millie said.

"They probably thought we were on our way back with something valuable," said Liam. "I wonder what Clarence told them to make them so interested in us."

"I don't know about Clarence, but I do know that you had a treasure with you," Audun said, glancing at Millie. "And I want to get her home right away. Oh, before I forget, here's the pearl, Annie. Sorry I can't stay to help you return it, but I really do want to get Millie home." The dragon reached into the pouch under his wing and pulled out the pearl.

"I don't blame you," Annie told him. She held up her hands, catching the pearl when he dropped it.

A moment later, Audun turned back into a human and reached for Millie. When he took the postcard of Greater Greensward out of his pocket, he glanced at Annie and Liam, saying, "We hope to see you again soon. Remember, you're always welcome to visit us, too."

"We will as soon as we can," said Liam.

"Thank you for all of your help!" Annie cried, and waved as their friends placed their fingers on the postcard and disappeared.

"How are your father and your uncle?" Liam asked, turning to Annie.

"Uncle Rupert was in bad shape when we got there, but he got better fast once he drank the potion," Annie replied. "I don't know if he would have lasted much longer if we hadn't given him the potion when we did. I'm really grateful to Audun for taking me to the castle."

"And your father?" asked Liam.

"He's fine now," Annie said. "He and Rupert had a big feast at noon today. I think they're trying to make up for all the meals they missed."

"That's great news! They have a real reason to celebrate," said Liam. "I've been thinking. Now that we know they're all right, we have no reason to hurry back. I'd like to go straight to Dorinocco, if you don't mind. We're so far south already, and we could get my mother and deal with her and the pearl that much sooner."

"That's a good idea," said Annie. "I just wish we had a postcard for Dorinocco. We'd be there in an instant."

"Maybe we'll have to make another trip to the Magic Marketplace," Liam replied. "They might have more postcards when we go back."

"And more singing swords," Annie said with a laugh. "I know how much you wanted one!"

"If we start now, we should reach the castle in Dorinocco before dark," Liam said as he helped Annie into the carriage. "We could go to the witches' island early tomorrow morning."

"That sounds good to me," said Annie. "I'd like to get the pearl to the monster as soon as we can. I feel like it's a hurdle I have to get past before we can really relax."

"That's exactly how I feel about taking my mother to the island," Liam told her. "The sooner we can get it done, the better!"

❧

King Montague was just sitting down to dinner in one of the smaller dining rooms when Annie and Liam arrived at the castle. "Excellent timing!" said the king. "I wasn't looking forward to eating alone, but now that you're here, I won't have to."

"You could always invite Mother to join you," Liam told him.

"Only if I wanted an argument instead of a conversation," said his father. "I'd prefer a conversation tonight, so I'm glad you're here. Are you staying or is this another quick visit?"

"A quick one, I'm afraid," said Liam. "We've actually come to pick up Mother and take her to an island very far from here."

"We'll be back to stay as soon as we've left her on the island and taken care of one other small errand," said Annie. "And then you and I will plan Liam's coronation celebration."

"Then I suppose I should write my abdication speech," the king told them. "I can't put it off any longer. I must admit, while I'm glad your mother will be leaving the castle, a part of me is going to miss her. She may be a vile woman, but she certainly has made life interesting."

"We'll be here to keep life interesting for you soon enough," said Liam.

"Yes, but sometimes it takes a good argument to stir the blood. Ah, look! We're having roast rabbit tonight. I hope there's more than one, because I'm hungry!"

Annie and Liam were both exhausted. Soon after the last course was served, Liam turned to his father. "If you'll excuse us, Annie and I would like to retire for the night. We had a long, hard day and tomorrow may be even worse."

"Then by all means, go get some rest," said the king. "I believe I'll do the same. I'd rather face your mother when I'm well rested. Dealing with her is always draining."

They all walked up the stairs together, but when they reached the top, the king went one way and Annie and Liam went the other. They trudged down the corridor to Liam's boyhood room in an older part of the castle. "We'll move to a bigger room after the coronation," Liam said as he opened the door.

Annie smiled when she stepped into the room. It was about the same size as the room that had been hers in her parents' castle, and it was filled with the kinds of things that young princes liked. A tapestry depicting a boy dressed in old-fashioned clothes walking through the woods with a dog was on one wall. An even larger tapestry with a picture of a unicorn and a lion nearly covered another wall. Crossed swords, both of which were badly nicked and battered, hung above the bed.

"Where is the magic mirror?" Annie asked. "I asked the men who brought it in to put it in the room I was going to use."

"I didn't want it spying on us all the time," said Liam. "I had them put it in a room down the corridor."

"But it's harmless!" said Annie.

"I didn't say it wasn't," Liam said. "I just don't want it in the room." Pulling her into his arms, Liam gave her a very tender kiss.

"Good thinking!" Annie finally said as Liam blew out the candles.

❦

Annie wasn't looking forward to seeing Lenore again, but she was just as anxious as Liam to get their trip to the island over. She was carrying a soft cloth bag with the pearl inside when she entered the small dining room. The king was already sitting down, and she took the seat beside him when he gestured to her. Liam had stopped to speak to a servant, but he joined Annie as soon as he had finished. The king was telling Annie what he planned to do that day when his wife appeared in the doorway and the conversation died.

Two guards flanked Queen Lenore as she strode into the room, looking as haughty as ever. When she reached the table, she scowled at Annie, who hadn't realized that she was sitting in the queen's seat.

"You may sit across from me," the king told Queen Lenore. "I want to be able to keep an eye on you."

"Because you think I'm so beautiful?" asked the queen, smirking.

The king shook his head. "No, because I don't trust you."

"Why did you send for me, Montague? You haven't requested my presence in nearly a week."

"He sent for you because I asked him to," Liam said as he joined them at the table. "Enjoy your breakfast and I'll tell you all about it when we've finished eating."

"Are you here to tell me about Clarence?" the queen asked, taking the seat across from the king.

"No, but I can if you'd like," said Liam. "He's embarked on a new career."

"What are you talking about?" demanded his mother. "Princes don't have careers. Except for you. As far as I can tell, your career is to ruin my life."

"Lenore!" chided the king.

"But it's true!" said the queen. "Clarence was a perfect baby. He slept through the night from the day he was born. When he was a little boy, he always listened to me and did everything I told him to do. You were a fretful infant, a bratty little boy, and an impossible young man. If only you had gone off to sea and stayed there!"

"Speaking of going off to sea," said Liam. "We took

Clarence to a faraway land where he can't cause any trouble. As far as I'm concerned, that's perfect!"

The queen glared at Liam. "And how long are you going to keep him exiled to this faraway land where he's supposed to engage in this career?"

Liam smiled as he leaned toward his mother. "Forever! Now I really do suggest you eat. It may be the last time you have a meal like this."

"What do you mean by that?" asked the queen. "Are you sending me into exile as well?"

"No," Liam said, looking serious. "I'm not sending you anywhere. Annie and I are taking you there."

"If you're taking me to that dreadful tower where you locked up Granny Bentbone, you should know right now that I refuse to go," the queen said as she reached for her cup.

"I wouldn't dream of taking you there!" said Liam. "That's much too close. Now eat your breakfast and I'll tell you what I have planned for you as soon as we've finished eating. Not another question until then!"

"Why does he get to decide my fate like this?" the queen said, turning to her husband.

"Like I told you before, I'm about to abdicate and he's going to be king. Now eat your breakfast! No more talking!"

Despite Liam's warning about future breakfasts, the queen picked at her food, and had eaten very little by the time everyone else had finished. "Are you ready?" Liam asked, turning to Annie.

She nodded and took his hand when he offered it. "Let's get this over with," she told him.

The servants had brought in a large crate and a small trunk, placing them just inside the door. "You need to join us, Mother," Liam said as he led Annie to the crate.

"I've decided that I'm not going anywhere," said the queen.

When Liam motioned to the guards, they each placed a hand under her arms and lifted her from her chair. "Let me go!" she shouted, trying to squirm free.

"Annie, this should work if you sit on the crate and hold the strap with one hand and place your other hand on my arm. Mother, stand beside me and hold this," Liam said, handing her the small trunk.

"This is heavy!" exclaimed the queen. "Just where do you think you're taking me?"

"To the witches' island," said Liam as he made a show of taking the medallion out of his shirt.

"It's a beautiful tropical island where a group of witches live," explained Annie.

Annie noticed that when Liam took hold of his mother's hand, he stuck his free hand in the pocket where he'd placed the postcard of the island. "What?" screeched his mother. "I'm not going to any island with witches. You can't possibly believe that I would spend any time with a group of old hags, let alone live there!"

The queen was still ranting about witches when Liam touched the postcard and they disappeared.

CHAPTER 17

ANNIE, LIAM, AND QUEEN LENORE found themselves on the sandy shore of a tropical island. Waves broke on the beach in front of them while tropical birds called out in the frond-topped trees behind them. Annie was pleased to see that the crate and trunk had also arrived.

"No!" wailed the queen, jerking her hand out of Liam's grip. "I am not staying here! You take me back to my castle this instant! How dare you treat me like this! I am your queen and your mother!"

"What's going on here?" a short, plump woman asked from a path that led into the trees. "Who are you people? Why is that woman screeching?"

"Norelle, isn't it?" said Liam, turning to face her. "I don't know if you remember me ..."

"I do now that you've turned around!" said the woman. "Did you go to Greater Greensward? You aren't still looking for a way to get home, are you?"

"No, no! We're fine. We went to Greater Greensward and they were able to help us. We're back because I'd like my mother to live here with you."

"Is she a witch? We don't let just anyone stay here," said Norelle. "We're a very select group. I think we need to go to the village so you can explain yourself to everyone."

"No, I'm not a witch!" cried Queen Lenore. "I don't belong here! I'm a queen. I can't live on an island with witches!"

"Oh, really? Think you're too good for us, do you?" said Norelle. "Follow me. I want you to meet my friends."

"What about the crate and the trunk?" Annie asked Liam, but it was Norelle who answered.

"I'll take care of that!" the little witch said. Pointing at the crate, she muttered a few words. The crate wobbled back and forth, but didn't go anywhere.

"Why isn't this working?" Norelle said to herself. Frowning, she stared at her fingertip as if the answer might be written there.

Annie glanced down. Her leg was touching the crate. "Uh, it was probably me again. Remember how magic doesn't work on me? It doesn't work on anything or anyone I'm touching, either. The last time I was here, Hennah's spell bounced off me and tossed her into the ocean."

"I remember that! We still get a good chuckle when we talk about it!"

"Look, I'll go over here so you can try again," said Annie.

"All right. Nope, nope, a little farther just to be sure. All right now. Let's try this again." Pointing her finger at the crate and trunk, the witch said a few words. Both objects disappeared in a bright flash of light. "Did you see that?" cried Norelle. "The old girl hasn't lost it yet!"

"Very impressive," said Liam.

"You bet it is!" Norelle exclaimed. "Now follow me and we'll be there before you can say my full name backward five times!"

"But we don't know your full name," said Annie.

Norelle chortled and grinned at Annie. "Exactly!"

Annie and Liam followed Norelle across the sand into the trees with Lenore trailing behind. Annie wasn't concerned that the queen would run off. It was a small island and from what she had seen during their last visit, there really wasn't anywhere to hide. It wasn't long before they were passing a freshwater pond that marked the center of the island. Minutes later they emerged into the sunlight to find a cluster of grass huts roofed with fronds from the trees.

"What did you find, Norelle?" shouted a tall woman with a sour expression.

"Did you send this stuff here?" asked a surly-looking

woman. "It almost clobbered me when I was on my way to the pond." She kicked the crate, apparently forgetting that she was barefoot. Swearing, she began to hop on the other foot while cradling the sore foot in her hand.

"Sorry, Hennah," said Norelle. "That stuff belongs to these people. I brought them here so they could tell all of you what they were telling me. I found them on the other side of the island and this one was yelling her head off." She pointed at Lenore, who looked like she'd rather be anywhere but there. "She says she's a queen."

"What were you yelling about? Were you having a fight?" asked a tall, thin witch with a long face and a narrow nose. "I like good fights. I can watch if you want an audience."

"We're here because I want my mother to live with you ladies," said Liam. "I'm banishing her from my kingdom, and I'd appreciate it if she could stay here with you."

"Why would we want her here? If she's a queen, she's going to expect to boss us around," said the tall witch.

"Yes, I will!" cried Lenore. "I'll tell you what to do every minute of the day. You'd hate having me here."

"When I first saw them, Queenie there was saying how much she didn't want to live with the likes of us," said Norelle.

"What makes you think we'd let her live with us?" asked a woman with long, curling white hair. "How do you know we wouldn't just pitch her in the water and let her drown?"

"Because I brought this," Liam said. Using his knife, he pried open the hasp that kept the crate closed and lifted the lid. Inside was a side of beef, a slab of cured bacon, and a collection of new pots and pans. "If you let my mother stay here with you, and don't let her leave, I'll bring you more food every month."

"Including more bacon? I love bacon!" cried Hennah.

"Including more bacon," said Liam.

"Good!" Hennah declared. "'Cause I'd do anything for bacon!"

"You're going to say yes just because he's trying to bribe us with food?" asked Rugene.

"I sure am!" said Hennah.

"Sounds good to me!" Rugene announced. "I'm getting real tired of fish! But she's going to have to make her own hut and help out with the chores. Just because she's a queen doesn't mean she'll get special treatment."

When the others nodded, Annie had a feeling that Liam had won his case. But then Lenore started talking and Annie wasn't quite as sure. "I don't care if you'd let me live here," the queen cried. "This place is terrible! The only buildings are run-down shacks that are probably vermin-infested or worse. And I'm not going to spend the rest of my life with a bunch of snaggletoothed hags who wouldn't know a hairbrush if it swatted them on their backsides!"

"That's not fair!" said Norelle. "Cadmilla brushes her hair two hundred times every day."

"And yet she lives in a hovel!" shouted Lenore. "I demand that you take me home right now, Liam! For once in your life, do what I say!"

"Sorry, Mother," said Liam. "You lost any right to tell me what to do a long time ago."

Lenore's face was turning red when she cried, "You always were an ungrateful wretch!"

"And you were always a terrible mother," Liam said, and turned back to the witches. Although Norelle looked distressed about the exchange between mother and son, the other witches appeared to be gleeful.

"That's exactly how my daughter used to talk to me!" said Rugene. "I miss it. Maybe I shouldn't have turned her into a muskrat the last time I saw her. I wonder where she is now?"

"Would any of you ladies happen to know where the sea monster lives?" asked Liam.

"Which one?" said Norelle. "At least five live around here."

Annie tried to remember everything that Pearl had told her about the monster. "We're looking for one with short arms, a pronged tail, and a tall fin on its back. Have any of you seen one like that?"

"I think I saw one that looks like that by the big drop-off," said Hennah.

"Don't listen to her," said Norelle. "She'll tell you that it went over the drop-off and want you to follow it."

"It did go over the drop-off!" Hennah cried.

"A monster like that used to live in the coral reef," said another witch. "But that was before Emma stole the pearl for Nastia Nautica."

"I passed it in the seaweed bed just last week," said another. "It scared me half to death when it popped out of the weeds. That thing has a mouth like a cave! I thought it was going to swallow me whole."

"I think it lives on the far side of Nastia Nautica's old sunken ship."

"You're wrong! That monster left after Emma stole its pearl! I haven't seen it since!"

Hennah shook her head. "You see why I don't tell the truth very often? Nobody believes me when I do. Might as well make something up, I say to myself. But not this time. That monster went over the drop-off slick as a slug slipping over the edge of a water barrel. Its pronged tail was the last thing I saw of it. Pretty thing if you ask me."

Liam and Annie gave each other a look. None of this was very helpful because they didn't know whom to believe. "Thank you, ladies," Liam told the witches. "You've given us plenty of places to look."

"How are you going to look for a sea monster? You don't have gills," said Rugene.

"And magic doesn't work on you," Norelle said to Annie.

Liam smiled. "We have our ways." Turning to Annie, he asked, "Are you ready?"

Annie nodded. "Let's see if we can get this done today." Taking Liam's hand, she started toward the water. She used her free hand to pat the amulet hidden beneath the neck of her gown, reassuring herself that it was there.

The witches followed them to the water's edge, arguing among themselves about how Annie and Liam were going to survive without air.

"Maybe she's really a mermaid," said one witch.

"Or they have a giant bubble waiting for them just out of sight," said another.

Remembering how difficult it had been to swim from Pearl's shipwreck while fully dressed in a long gown and shoes, Annie thought about taking off her clothes so she could swim in her undergarments. Norelle seemed to be the nicest of the witches, and Annie could ask her to watch over their clothes and shoes and…Annie shook her head. She didn't know what Norelle was really like. The postcards were in Liam's pocket and she didn't trust anyone else with them. Glancing at the witches, Annie decided that she shouldn't trust any of them. She certainly wasn't about to ask Lenore, who was sitting on the crate, pouting.

Although Annie knew how well Audun's amulet

had worked before, she still felt uneasy as the waves washed over her feet and up her legs. What if the amulet didn't work this time? What if she took her first breath and her lungs filled with water? Faced with the vastness of the sea, the little amulet didn't seem like much protection.

"Good luck!" Norelle called.

"Yeah," shouted Hennah. "Good luck and don't let the sea monsters bite!"

The other witches must have given Hennah a funny look, because she paused and said, "What? I want more bacon and I won't get it if a sea monster eats them!"

CHAPTER 18

ANNIE AND LIAM had nearly reached the point where the waves broke when they stopped and glanced at each other. Annie nodded and they dove into the heart of the next wave, still holding hands. As the ocean floor dropped lower, they followed it down.

Swimming underwater meant that they didn't have to fight the waves, but using one hand to hold on to Liam made swimming that much harder. They swam side by side until Annie's arms ached and she wasn't sure she could go much farther.

"Just a little more," said Liam, as if sensing Annie's fatigue. "Pearl said we should swim straight out for four hundred yards, and we're almost there. I've been keeping track; we should turn in a little while."

A large sea turtle swam past, surprising them both. Suddenly, Annie was worried about more than just the amulet not working or the sea monster lurking some-where in the ocean's depths. Now she had to worry about what else might be down there. The witches had said that there were five sea monsters in the area. And what about the fish? She had seen fish as long as boats when Millie carried her to the ice-dragon stronghold and had heard about fish with very sharp teeth and equally big appetites. The water was clear enough that she could see for a very long way, but what good would that do if a fish or sea monster was a faster swimmer?

Annie was looking around her when Liam tugged on her hand. It was time to change direction. Soon they could start looking for the castle that was their first landmark. They should probably start looking for the sea monster now, though. They were going to look in certain places, but it might be anywhere, even right below them. At that thought, Annie glanced down, then quickly looked behind her. The sea mon-ster wasn't anywhere in sight, but that didn't mean it wasn't close by.

"There it is!" Liam finally exclaimed. Annie thought he meant the monster until she spotted the castle lying right in front of them. The castle was made of coral with wide windows and a shell door at ground level. Tall spires rose about the castle, and Annie was sure she saw pennants made of seaweed.

"Both Millie and Pearl said that Coral lives there.

Should we stop and ask her if she's seen the monster?" asked Annie.

"There's no need," said Liam. "Pearl gave us good directions."

"But Coral might have seen the monster recently and could give us an idea where we should look first."

Liam shook his head. "We don't need to. I can handle this."

Annie sighed, but she didn't ask again. If Liam didn't want to go, there wasn't much she could do to change his mind.

They swam past the castle, heading for the wall of seaweed that they could just make out beyond it. The seaweed was tall, reaching from the ocean floor to just below the waves. As they got closer, they saw that it was also dense; each strand was at least a foot wide. Anything hidden in its depths would be nearly impossible to find. It reminded Annie of a regular forest, but unlike trees with sturdy trunks that didn't move, every bit of the seaweed plants undulated in the ocean's current, endlessly swaying back and forth.

"I hope we don't run into the monster in here," Annie said as they neared the forest.

"I hope we don't run into *anything* in here," said Liam.

They tried to swim side by side, but the seaweed made it difficult. After a little experimentation, they ended up with Annie holding on to Liam's shoulders as he pulled her through the plants.

Annie was lost before they'd gone a few yards into the seaweed. She was sure that if she were leading the way, they would be going in circles. Liam, however, seemed to be able to go in a straight line and was moving right along when suddenly they were in a cloud of tiny fish. Faster than the blink of an eye, the fish changed direction, going back the way they had come.

Liam turned his head to glance at Annie. "Did you see that?" he asked.

"I did!" Annie replied. "I didn't know that fish could move that fast."

"I didn't know anything could," said Liam.

They continued on, encountering a few curious fish and a pair of delicate sea horses that seemed to be playing tag. Annie was wondering if they would ever get through the forest when Liam pushed aside a wide strand of seaweed and came face-to-face with an enormous eel. The eel's head was as wide as Annie's arm and had eyes that looked as big as her fist. Annie thought it must be almost as big as a dragon. When she let out a small shriek, the creature turned and fled, swaying the seaweed on one side, then the other as its tail swept back and forth.

"I think you startled him," said Liam.

"Thank goodness!" Annie replied. "I don't know what we would have done if he'd stuck around."

"I really don't like this," Liam said as he started swimming again. "I hope we get out of here soon."

"Are you sure we're going straight?" asked Annie.

"As sure as I can be," Liam told her.

In only a few more minutes, Liam pushed past one more strand and they found themselves in the open. Annie sighed with relief as she let go of his shoulders and took his hand so she could swim beside him. "Isn't that the shipwreck over there?" she asked, spying something with a vaguely shiplike shape.

"It might be," said Liam. "It's hard to tell with all that coral growing on it."

When they swam closer, they found that it was a shipwreck nearly covered in coral. Fish darted in and out of gaping holes in the ship, and Annie spotted at least three sea snakes when she peeked inside. "Millie said that this was where Nastia Nautica used to live. I wonder if it was this bad when she lived here."

"There's one good thing about all these holes," Liam noted. "You can see all the way through. I don't see any monsters yet. I guess we should go in to look around."

"Not with sea snakes in there!" cried Annie.

Liam turned to argue with Annie, but stopped when he saw something behind her. "Annie, watch out! A little sea monster is coming right at us and it's got a knife!"

Annie spun around and saw the creature facing her from only a few feet away. Mottled skin covered a sack-like body and eight long tentacle arms, one of which was brandishing a knife at her.

"Put that knife down, Octavius!" called a melodious voice. "Can't you see they're humans?"

The monster's eyes swiveled toward a beautiful mermaid with silver and dark blue hair. The arm holding the knife drooped as the creature backed away.

"You can talk to the monster?" Annie asked her.

The mermaid laughed, a bright, happy sound that made Annie smile. "Octavius isn't a monster! He's an octopus and my butler. He believes that he's my protector as well, although I really can take care of myself."

"Is your name Coral?" Annie asked her. "My friend Millie told me that was the name of a mermaid who lives around here."

"You know Millie! How is she? I haven't seen her in ages!"

"She's doing well," said Annie. "She and Audun are expecting their first baby."

"That's wonderful! I'm sure Emma and Eadric are thrilled. I know that ... Octavius, put that knife away. It's obvious that these people aren't going to try to hurt me. In fact, you can go back to the castle now. I believe we've solved the mystery of the two-headed monster."

"There's a two-headed monster here?" asked Liam as the octopus scuttled away.

Coral laughed again. "If I'm right, *you* were the two-headed monster. Did you swim close together when you came through the seaweed?"

215

Annie nodded. "Liam swam while I held on to his shoulders."

"Then that explains it!" cried Coral. "At least half a dozen fish came to tell me that there was a monster with two heads in the seaweed today. Octavius and I came to scare it away if necessary." She held up a long tube that didn't appear to be at all threatening. "It may not look like much, but it can knock a three-thousand-pound sea monster from here to tomorrow. If you don't mind my asking, why are you here?"

"We've come looking for a sea monster," said Annie. "Do you know of one with a pronged tail and a tall back fin?"

"Don't forget the monster's short arms," said Liam.

"Of course!" said Coral. "That would be Old Warty. Why do you want to find him?"

"We want to return something that belongs to him," said Annie. "We wanted to do it anyway, but then we met a sea witch named Pearl. She thought it was a good idea, too."

"You know Pearl! She was one of my best friends. We used to do everything together until she ran away from her horrible mother. Where did you see her?"

"On the other side of the world," said Annie. "Her mother is there, too, so Pearl said she has to move again."

"Let me guess," Coral said. "You want to return the giant pearl to Old Warty. Don't look so surprised! It's

216

the only thing that monster has ever lost. I think it's a wonderful idea! Maybe I can help you. Just a minute."

Turning away from the shipwreck, the mermaid cupped her hands around her mouth and made high-pitched squeaks that ended in a long, drawn-out squeal. A moment later, a school of fish emerged from the sea-weed and swam straight to Coral. The mermaid made a few soft sounds, and the fish swam back into the forest.

"We should have some information for you in a few minutes," Coral told Annie and Liam. "Now, when you find Old Warty, you need to be careful. He's been very grumpy ever since Emma stole the pearl for Nasty Nautica."

"Oh, but she wasn't the one who had it," said Annie. "Emma gave it to Pearl, who took it with her when she ran away. We got it from Pearl, who was trying to keep it from her mother."

"Really! That's marvelous!" the mermaid exclaimed.

"And now we're giving it back to the sea monster for safekeeping."

"I'm sure it will make Old Warty happy to have it back," said Coral. "Ah, here are my helpers now. Let's see what they learned."

Although Annie strained to hear what the fish were saying to the mermaid, she didn't hear much other than the normal sounds of the ocean. They must have said something, however, because Coral replied with a small squeak and the fish all swam away.

"They say that Old Warty is napping in the seaweed, but should be waking soon. He usually heads into the drop-off after his nap. If you want to give the pearl back, you need to do it now. The pressure in the drop-off is too much for you and it's so dark, you wouldn't be able to see a thing."

"Could the fish show us the way to Old Warty?" asked Liam.

"There's no need to ask them," said Coral. "They told me where he is, so I can show you."

Annie held on to Liam's shoulders again as he followed the mermaid into the seaweed forest. Although Coral didn't take the same route that Liam had, it all looked the same to Annie. They had been swimming for a while when Octavius appeared, using all eight of his arms to shove the seaweed aside and force his way through. Coral turned, tilting her head as if she was listening. She looked upset when she faced Annie and Liam again. "The witches from the island are back. They come down here now and then and get into trouble every time. I'm sorry, but I'm afraid that I have to go. I need to stop them from doing whatever they have planned. Look, Old Warty is straight ahead, right through there," she said, pointing. "Just be careful. He's always grumpy, but he's even grumpier when he wakes up from a nap."

"Thank you for your help!" Annie told her.

"You're welcome," Coral replied. "I'm just sorry I

couldn't go with you to give the pearl back. Old Warty might be more cooperative if I was there. Ah, well. It can't be helped. Good luck!"

"A grumpy sea monster," Liam muttered as Coral swam away. "Can this get any better?" Shaking his head, Liam started swimming again. He hadn't gone far when the seaweed in front of them bent and swirled as if something big had swum past.

"Hurry!" cried Annie. "Old Warty must be leaving."

A few yards farther and they were in a tunnel of flattened seaweed. Annie could just make out a tail disappearing into the still-standing plants ahead of them. The prongs on the tail were so big that the monster had to be enormous; the path that the monster left in the seaweed was wide enough for Annie and Liam to swim side by side again.

They followed the monster all the way to the edge of the forest. As soon as they were free of the seaweed, they were able to see the entire monster. Annie hadn't expected him to be pretty, but no one had said how ugly he looked. Most of his leatherlike skin was covered with barnacles, giving him a prickly appearance. The fin on his back had jagged edges, and his pronged tail was thick and stumpy. Although Annie and Liam tried to swim around the creature, they couldn't seem to pass him no matter how hard they tried.

"I think I see the drop-off," Liam said after a while. "See there, where the ocean floor seems to end."

"We can't let him reach the drop-off!" Annie cried. "There must be something we can do to stop him!"

"Yoo-hoo!" cried a voice from overhead. A giant bubble was falling through the water. When Annie and Liam realized that it was headed straight for them, they had to dive to the side to get out of its way. The five witches inside waved at them. "We came to see how you're doing!" shouted Hennah.

The bubble hit the ocean floor and bounced, sending the witches inside flying back and forth from one side to the other like kernels of corn in hot oil. As the bubble rose again, they rolled around in a jumble of arms and legs, trying to get themselves sorted out. When it came down the next time, it hit Old Warty squarely on his back.

The sea monster had been about to slip over the edge of the drop-off. Startled, he roared and turned around. For the first time, Annie was able to see his blunt nose and little squidgy eyes. Because the bubble was already on its way up again, he didn't see the witches. Instead, his eyes landed on Annie and Liam, the only others who were there.

Liam jerked on Annie's arm, tugging her backward as the sea monster lunged at them. Suddenly the bubble was back, slamming into the monster's head. Enraged, Old Warty shook himself and roared again, opening his mouth so wide that Annie and Liam could see halfway down his throat.

"Annie, give me the pearl!" shouted Liam.

Annie hurriedly took it from the bag and handed it to him. "You don't mean to go in his mouth, do you?" she asked as Liam started to drag them closer.

The monster blinked. Spotting Annie and Liam, he started toward them again.

"Not at all," Liam said. "But it would help if he roared now."

This time Old Warty was only yards from Annie and Liam when the bubble started down. Hennah was lying on the floor of the bubble, her face plastered to the inside, when she saw what Liam was holding. The bubble bounced off Old Warty's nose and she flew up, already screaming, "They've got the giant pearl!"

The monster roared again, opening his mouth even wider.

"Stay here," Liam told Annie, and let go of her hand. Holding his breath, he launched himself at the sea monster. As Old Warty started to close his mouth, Liam tossed the pearl in, flipped over, and pushed off from the monster's lower lip. The pearl hit the top of the monster's throat. Old Warty's mouth snapped shut and his eyes widened in surprise. Suddenly his face developed a dreamy look. With his eyes half-closed, he turned and headed back to the drop-off, ignoring the bubble when it hit his tail and bounced toward Annie. She watched as he slipped over the edge. With a flick of his pronged tail, he was gone.

Liam had almost reached Annie again when she saw that the bubble was about to hit them. There wasn't time to do more than grab Liam's hand. When the bubble slammed into them, it sent them sprawling into the soft silt of the ocean bottom. Even that moment of contact with Annie was enough to weaken the strength of the spell holding the bubble intact. It popped, and the witches tumbled in five different directions.

Annie sat up, dazed. When she started to regain her senses, she was happy to see that she was still holding Liam's hand. A moment later she noticed the witches floundering in the water. "Liam, they're going to drown!" she cried.

"I don't think so," said Liam. "Watch."

A yellow light was already glowing around Hennah. Suddenly something yellow and shiny enveloped her, and began to rise to the surface like a drop of oil in a pan of water. A sea turtle arrived to carry one of the witches to the surface, while the others made their own bubbles so they could float up.

"It's time to go home," said Liam. He turned his head as Coral swam to them, looking worried.

"Are you all right?" asked the mermaid.

"We're fine," said Annie. "We did what we came to do and no one got hurt."

"I didn't see everything, but I did see the look on Old Warty's face after you tossed the pearl into his mouth," said Coral. "He already looked sleepy. I've always suspected that it was the pearl that helped him sleep so long."

"Talk about sleeping!" Annie said, stifling a yawn. "I don't know if I have enough energy to swim all the way back to the island."

"I can help with that!" Coral told her. Once again the mermaid cupped her hands around her mouth and made high squealing sounds. This time a porpoise came out of the seaweed forest and swam up to Coral.

"Sala will take you to the island faster than you could swim there," said Coral. "I'm glad I got to meet you both. Say hi to Millie and Audun for me when you see them. And if you ever see Pearl again, please tell her that I miss her!"

"We will," said Annie. "Thank you for all your help."

"It was my pleasure!" Coral replied. "Any friend of Millie's is a friend of mine!"

At a nod from Coral, Sala, the porpoise, swam between Annie and Liam. "Hold on tight," the mermaid told them as they took hold of the fin on Sala's back. "She's awfully fast!"

"We will...," Liam began, but then the porpoise took off and all Annie and Liam could do was hold on.

They reached the island only minutes later. Annie was enjoying it so much that she wished the trip could have lasted longer. Sala took them to the unoccupied side of the island, letting them off only feet from the shore. When they were standing beside her, she squealed, sounding just like Coral, waved her flipper at them, and headed back into deeper water.

"I suppose we should go say good-bye to the witches and your mother," Annie said as they waded out of the water.

"If we must," Liam said with a sigh. "The less I see of my mother, the happier I'll be."

"Then you should be overjoyed very soon," Annie told him. "Although we will have to bring more bacon in a month."

"Mustn't forget the bacon!" Liam said with a laugh. "Who knows what Hennah would do if we didn't bring it!"

They took the shortcut through the middle of the island and were approaching the witches' huts when they heard the women talking.

"It's a real shame that they gave that pearl back to the sea monster," said a witch.

"It's not a shame! It's a disaster!" cried Hennah. "Do you know what I could have done with that thing?"

"No, what?" asked another witch.

"I don't know," said Hennah. "I was asking you! Say, Lenny, why don't you build your hut over here. I think you and I are going to be good friends."

"My name is Queen Lenore!" announced Liam's mother.

224

"Yeah, like I said—Lenny! Come on, I'll show you where you can get some good palm fronds for your hut."

"What are palm fronds?" asked the queen.

"Boy, do I have a lot to teach you!" Hennah told her.

"I think we should leave," Liam whispered to Annie as he led her back among the trees. "I don't want to run into either of them right now. Here's the postcard for Treecrest."

"It will be nice to go to one place and stay there for a while," said Annie. "I'm awfully tired of traveling. If only we had a card for Dorinocco. It would be so much simpler if we could go directly there instead of always having to go to Treecrest first. I love seeing my parents, but we'll have to travel another day to get to Dorinocco."

"I'm not sure how I feel about the postcards," said Liam. "Sure, they make it easier to get around, but I hate to think what could happen if they fell into the wrong hands. Some of the people we saw at the Magic Marketplace are not the kind we want showing up at the castle. Would you really want someone like Hennah dropping in for a visit?"

"I suppose you're right," said Annie. "But just think how much easier it would be if our friends had postcards for Dorinocco."

"So they could visit us more often?" asked Liam.

"So they could come to your coronation!" Annie exclaimed. "Now that my relatives are healthy and yours can't make any more trouble for us, it's time to plan the biggest celebration ever! If our guests use the post-cards, we won't have to worry that they might get lost or bandits might waylay them. Our only concerns will be getting the ceremony exactly right, what food to serve, and where the guests will sleep when they get there."

Liam shook his head. "There is one other thing that worries me. With all those people at our castle, how am I going to find time to do this?" he said, and bent down for a kiss.

It was a long and very enjoyable kiss. When it was over, Annie gazed into Liam's eyes long enough to say, "I'm sure we'll find a way!" before returning for another.

The magic continues in the Wide-Awake Princess series!

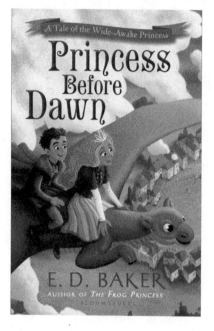

Princess Annie's beloved Treecest has become a favorite destination for all sorts of magical beings. One new set of guests is particularly strange, and they are ready to take over a new hunting ground. Annie and Liam turn to their only friends who can help, Francis and Zoe. Can they figure out a way to reclaim Treecrest before it's overrun with hunters? Or will Annie lose her one true home?

TWO WEEKS HAD passed since Annie and Liam had returned the pearl to the sea monster. After coming home to Dorinocco, planning their coronation had taken up nearly all their time.

"I really wish you hadn't invited all the fairies from Treecrest *and* Dorinocco to the coronation," Liam told Annie as they ate their breakfast in the sunlit private dining room. "You know how much trouble fairies can make, and there will be so many of them!"

Edda, Annie's troll dog, looked up at her adoringly. The enormous dog had put her head in Annie's lap as soon as they sat down. Annie scratched Edda behind the ears, then slipped a piece of sausage to her. "They'd make even more trouble if I hadn't invited them. Remember what happened with our first wedding?" Annie said to Liam. "They ruined it when they thought we hadn't sent them invitations."

"Thanks to Squidge," Liam muttered as he reached for another pastry.

"Did someone call my name?" the little sprite said, appearing in the doorway.

Annie blinked in surprise as he stepped into the room and climbed onto an empty chair. "Did you show up because Liam said your name?" she asked.

Squidge chuckled. "Names are powerful things and you should never say them unless you're willing to face the consequences." He was grinning when he looked at Annie's and Liam's incredulous faces. When he opened his mouth again, he had a twinkle in his eyes, but he seemed to rethink whatever he was going to say and sighed instead. "I could tell you that Liam called me by saying my name—and I bet I could get you to believe it—but I promised the fairies that I'd behave. They are such spoilsports lately."

"What are you talking about?" asked Liam.

"The fairies actually sent me here to help you plan your coronation," the sprite explained. "They said I owed you community service and that I had to do whatever you wanted."

"And why should we trust you?" Liam asked, frowning.

"Because they said they'd turn me into a gnat if I made any more mischief. I hate gnats and they know it."

"What if we say we don't need your help?" Annie asked him.

Squidge shrugged. "Of course you need my help. I can do all sorts of things that you can't. I was very useful when I helped you get ready for your wedding. Remember how I washed all the dogs and scrubbed the dungeon steps and—"

"Didn't send out the invitations when you told us you had?" said Annie. "Yes, we remember."

"I won't sabotage it this time. I promise!" Squidge exclaimed. "Now tell me, what do you have planned so far?"

"Don't tell him," Liam said to Annie.

"I don't know if it matters," she replied. "He'd find out anyway. We're going to have a traditional ceremony, then the feast and coronation ball. We were just about to discuss the menu before you popped up."

"Good! I like talking about food, although I like eating it even more," Squidge said, eyeing the food on the table. "Can you pass me some of those pastries? I'm about to faint from hunger."

There was a knock on the door and a footman peeked in. "Your Majesties, a fairy just dropped off a message from the king and queen of Treecrest."

"What do you suppose your parents want?" Liam said to Annie. "We were there just a few weeks ago."

"I'll take it," Annie told the footman.

He hurried into the room and handed her a folded slip of parchment, then bowed and left.

"Oh, dear," Annie said when she'd read it. "This can't

be good. They said that they need our help and want us to come right away. It's an emergency. The castle is overrun with uninvited guests who refuse to leave."

"How is that an emergency?" asked Liam.

"I suppose that depends on the guests," said Annie. "I can get ready immediately, but we need to tell your father."

"I'm going, too!" Squidge cried as Annie and Liam stood.

Annie shook her head. "I don't think so. You haven't done anything to make me think we can trust you."

"What if I polish everyone's shoes?" said the sprite. "Or give you flowers every day? Or pick the fleas off all the dogs?"

"You could start by apologizing," Liam told him. "And then work at being good as hard as you worked at being bad."

"I'm sorry, I'm sorry, I'm sorry times a hundred billion, gajillion times!" Squidge cried, clasping his hands in front of him. "Will you ever forgive me?"

"Only if you truly behave yourself!" Annie warned him.

"I'll be as good as gold!" Squidge declared. "No, make that as good as a gooseberry pie! They're my favorite. But I should really have a few more of those pastries before I go anywhere."

᠅

"Uninvited guests?" King Montague said, rubbing his leg that was hurting from gout again. Annie and Liam had gone to see Liam's father to tell him that they would be away for a day or so. "That could mean anything from enemy soldiers at the gates to bedbugs in the linens. Neither one is good. Would you like me to send some knights with you just in case?"

"The message didn't say it was an invasion, so I don't think we'll need any knights," said Liam. "But thank you for the offer. Besides, Annie and I are traveling by postcard. We'll be in Treecrest moments after we leave here. Traveling with knights would take us too long. Whatever the problem is, we hope to settle it quickly and get back here as soon as possible. We've already told everyone what they need to do to prepare for the coronation."

"I'll make sure they keep working on it," his father replied. "And I'll keep Edda here with me. We get along just fine, don't we, girl?" Summoning the dog by patting his gouty leg, the king grimaced when it hurt.

Edda left Annie's side and lumbered over to sit beside Montague, who immediately started petting her.

"Is there anything else you need me to do?" he asked Annie and Liam.

"Just rest and take care of your leg. I'd like to dance with you at least once at the coronation ball," Annie said, and kissed him on the cheek before she left with Liam.

"THIS SHOULD BE FUN!" Squidge exclaimed. "I've never traveled by postcard before. What do I have to do?"

Annie smiled at Liam. They had traveled by magic postcard so many times by now that it was no longer as exciting as it had been at first. Having someone with them who had never traveled that way before was fun, even if it was the annoying little sprite.

"Nothing," Annie said as she picked him up and reached for Liam's hand.

The sprite had joined them in the king's audience chamber just moments before. His pockets were bulging with pastries and he had icing on his chin and lips.

"I mean, should I hold my breath or close my eyes or stick my fingers in my nose and plug my ears or stand on my head and gargle or—"

Liam touched the postcard that he'd placed in his pocket. A moment later they were standing on the gravel road that led to the drawbridge, looking up at the castle where Annie had been born.

"Wow!" Squidge cried as Annie set him down. "That was fast! Can we do it again?"

"Not right now," Annie said, laughing. "It works only one way."

"We need to get more postcards. This sure beats tricking a rabbit into giving me a ride or calling up a wind to carry me. Say, I know that cat!" he said when he spotted a gray tabby at the edge of the moat. "Mind if I go say hello? I'll only be a minute. I'll see you later!"

The little sprite had run off to join his friend when something in the moat caught Annie's eye. "Do you see that?" she asked Liam, nudging him in the side. "There are people swimming in the moat!"

"Yuck! I'd never do that," Liam replied. "Granted, your moat is cleaner than most, but it's a long way from being safe enough to drink or to swim in. Who are those women?"

"No one from around here," Annie said, trying not to stare.

Four fully dressed women were swimming in the moat near the drawbridge. Their long hair streamed out behind them as they paddled from one side to the other, fouling the water with dirt and oil and turning it murky. The women were talking and laughing, their harsh cackles grating on Annie's nerves. "*These* must be the uninvited guests," she whispered to Liam.

"Watch out!" Liam cried, grabbing Annie's arm to stop her from walking into a man who had suddenly materialized in front of them. The man was shorter than Annie, and was wearing a bright blue cape over a dark blue tunic and leggings. He had stopped to tuck a magic postcard into a pocket when Annie almost stumbled to avoid him. The man barely spared them a glance over his shoulder as he headed to the drawbridge.

"I don't think those women are the only uninvited guests here today," Liam told Annie.

"It's those darn postcards!" Annie said as they followed the man to the castle courtyard. "I knew when I first saw them in the Magic Marketplace that they were going to create problems!"

Annie was already upset as they started across the drawbridge, but when she heard the ruckus and saw what lay beyond she was horrified. Strangers milled around the courtyard, getting in the way of the castle residents who were trying to go about their regular business. She saw a footman carrying a box unable to move because of the crowd around him. A stable boy couldn't reach the stable with the horse he was leading because of the people blocking him. Two knights trying to get to the guardhouse were stuck behind a group of wildly dressed men and women who were loudly criticizing the castle's architecture. These weren't the ordinary merchants who often came to the castle, nor were they visitors from any of Treecrest's neighbors. When Annie saw one wave a wand and turn the dovecote into a giant beehive, she knew exactly what they were.

Witches had used the magic postcards to come to Treecrest.

"I think I understand the problem now," she said to Liam through gritted teeth. "Let's go inside."

It took a while for Annie and Liam to work their way across the courtyard to the castle steps. Every time they saw an opening in the crowd, someone else would step up to fill it. Annie tried to be polite at first, saying "excuse me" even when someone bumped into her, but she finally began to lose patience and started pushing between people as she'd seen the strangers do.

When Annie was born, the fairy Moonbeam had given her the gift that no magic could touch her. This also meant that anyone else's magic didn't work when Annie was nearby. Even being close to Annie could diminish magic, although the effect wasn't permanent. None of the witches and wizards seemed to notice that their appearance changed or their magic no longer worked when Annie touched them. Even if they had, she was soon lost in the crowd and they couldn't have guessed that she was the reason for the change.

Walking up the castle steps proved to be just as difficult as crossing the courtyard. One old woman was sitting on the steps, pointing a wand at the sky. When

Annie looked up, she saw pigeons flying in circles over-head, following the movement of the wand. Everyone had to work their way around the woman, who didn't seem to know or care that she was in the way. A few steps higher, a man was juggling balls of light. When he dropped one, it landed on another man's shoulder. Although the light sputtered and went out, the second man turned around and shoved the juggler. Liam grabbed hold of Annie and dragged her through the crowd as the men started to fight, tossing spiders and sparks at each other.

The corridor inside wasn't quite as crowded, and Annie and Liam were able to make their way to the great hall without too much trouble. A statue of Captain Sterling, the captain of the guard, stood just inside the door. The statues of two of his men stood beside him. Someone had painted all three in bright splashes of blues, purples, and yellows, while someone else had wrapped the scarf from a lady's hat around the statue of the captain. Peeking around the statues, Annie saw that there appeared to be a party going on with a table set up for food at one end and a large group dancing to fiddle music in the middle. Witches and wizards stood in small groups, comparing notes on magic.

A witch standing by herself was popping bright red beans into her mouth, chewing them, then spit-ting them into a silver cup that Annie recognized as belonging to the royal family. The scent of something spicy was almost overwhelming when the witch opened her mouth, flashing teeth and gums as red as blood. As soon as the cup was full, the witch swirled its contents, muttered a few words, and poured it on the floor. The scarlet pulp turned into salamanders that scuttled off into the rushes.

"Look at all the food on that table!" Liam said as they made their way into the room. "It's enough to feed everyone in the entire castle for days! Do you suppose the cook made it or these people used a magic table-cloth like the animals from Bremen gave to Gwennie?"

"Good question," Annie said, shaking her head. The witches and wizards were gathered around the table as they picked at the roast boar, stuffed peacock, beef haunch, huge platter of fish, and mountain of pastries. Squidge and the gray tabby were there, too, helping themselves from the platters.

Annie and Liam were crossing the room when suddenly Liam began to dance to the music of the fiddle. "What are you doing?" Annie asked, surprised.

Liam looked confused as he exclaimed, "I don't know, but I can't help it!"

Annie glanced at the other people who were all dancing in the same way. Most of them had their backs to her as they faced the fiddle, but she thought one of them might work in the kitchen. The only person who seemed to be enjoying herself was the witch playing the fiddle. While Annie watched, the witch headed to the food-laden table while the fiddle hung in the air, still playing where she'd left it.

"Let's get out of here," Annie said, touching Liam's back.

As soon as the magic no longer controlled him, he stopped dancing with a sigh of relief and joined her as she headed for the door. "Thank you," he said. "I've never really liked dancing, especially like that."

"You're very welcome!" Annie told him with a smile. "I wonder how long those people have been dancing. The ones I saw looked awfully tired. Do you mind if we go to the kitchen? I want to see if Cook is making all that food. If she is, she'll use up all the stores and the buttery will be empty in days."

"Lead on," Liam said. "I'm curious, too."

Although they didn't hear the usual bustle and clang coming from the kitchen, they did hear two voices. When they peeked inside, neither Cook nor any of her helpers were there. Instead, two witches were stirring something that smelled like rancid fat in Cook's biggest pot while they compared recipes.

"I use the hair of the dog that bit me and the rag-weed that made me sneeze instead of henbane and bat ears," one witch said. "I find that personalizing a potion like that works better."

The second witch was mumbling something when Annie spotted Squidge in the corner, sharing a hunk of cheese with the gray tabby cat. The little sprite saw them and waved, but the cat didn't even look up.

"I've seen more than enough," Annie told Liam. "It's time we found my parents. I think I know what I have to do, but I want to talk to them first."

༄

They located Annie's parents in her father's chamber behind a locked and barricaded door. Annie had to assure them that she and Liam were alone before a footman would let them in. Once Annie and Liam were in the room, the servants locked the door and pushed a heavy table in front of it. Annie was surprised by how many people were there. All of her mother's ladies-in-waiting were crowded into the two rooms along with her father's attendants, half the guards, and at least a dozen servants.

"We thought everyone would be safer here with us than downstairs with those horrible people," the queen said when she saw Annie looking around in surprise.

"You do realize that 'those people' are witches and can probably go anywhere they want, right?" said Annie.

"I know, but we were hoping they'd leave us alone if they had the run of the rest of the castle," the queen replied.

Annie glanced at Liam. Her parents must be truly frightened to have given up the castle to strangers.

"I'm just glad that you and Liam got here safely," said the king. "We asked Captain Sterling to make the witches leave, but you saw what they did to him. Anyone who goes near the great hall now gets dragged into their dance. We didn't know what to do, so we sent for you hoping that you might have an idea. Your mother thought it best that we stay in my chambers until you arrived."

Annie nodded. "I wondered about those statues. Those poor men!"

"When did your 'uninvited guests' start arriving?" asked Liam.

"Yesterday morning," the queen told him. "It was just a few at first, but then one of them left and a few minutes later returned with a huge crowd. More have been coming ever since. We didn't know they were magic users until that horrible woman pointed her finger at the captain and his men, turning them to stone."

"And then that other witch made the scullery girls start dancing," added the king.

"They're still dancing," said Liam. "We saw them just a bit ago."

"The newcomers all looked like strangers," said Annie. "Am I right in saying that none of them came from around here?"

"As far as we know," said the queen. "No one in the castle recognized them. All these awful people in my castle! I don't know what we're going to do to make them leave."

"I do," Annie said, and headed for the door. "Let me out and barricade the door again. The party is over and it's time for those guests to go home."

"You're not going out there by yourself!" said Liam.

"Why not? They can't hurt me with their magic," Annie told him.

"Not directly, but if they use their magic on something else, it could hurt you," Liam replied. "Remember how Terobella sent the crows to hurt you and how she made the bridge collapse under your carriage? If you're leaving this room, I'm going with you."

"And you say I'm stubborn!" said Annie. "All right, but you have to let me do the talking."

ॐ

E. D. BAKER is the author of the Tales of the Frog Princess series, the Wide-Awake Princess series, the Fairy-Tale Matchmaker series, the Magic Animal Rescue series, and many other delightful books for young readers, including *A Question of Magic*, *Fairy Wings*, and *Fairy Lies*. Her first book, *The Frog Princess*, was the inspiration for Disney's hit movie *The Princess and the Frog*. She lives with her family and their many animals in Maryland.

Visit her online at www.talesofedbaker.com.

Be sure to join the mailing list for book announcements and special giveaways!